To: Jamie...

MONSTERS REALLY DO EXIST

David B Harrington

Schlock! Publications

Keep it... spooky!!
David Harrington

Copyright © 2022 David B Harrington

Schlock! Publications
www.schlock.co.uk

Edited by Gavin Chappell

All rights reserved.

No part of this publication may be reproduced, distributed, or transmitted in any form or by any means, including photocopying, recording, or other electronic or mechanical methods, without the prior written permission of the publisher, except in the case of brief quotations embodied in critical reviews and certain other noncommercial uses permitted by copyright law.

For permission requests, write to the publisher, addressed "Attention: Permissions Coordinator," at the web address above.

Any references to historical events, real people, or real places are used fictitiously. Names, characters, and places are products of the author's imagination.

ISBN (Paperback): 9798835738076
ISBN (Hardback): 9798835839216

Front cover image by Cameron Hampton.

Copyright © 2022 David B Harrington

All rights reserved. No part of this book may be reproduced or used in any manner without the prior written permission of the copyright owner, except for the use of brief quotations in a book review.

CONTENTS

Title Page
Copyright
Walrus in a Brothel   1
Salamander Springs   16
Girl on the #9 Bus   22
Madalyne Vandeveer   34
County Library   41
Salt Creek   51
Maggona Beach   60
Uncle Salty   70
Apparatus Hill   73
The Gravedigger   77
The Ghosts of Dragonhorn Manor   81
Metro Zoo   86

WALRUS IN A BROTHEL

Not all little girls are made of sugar and spice and everything nice.

As janitor of Our Lady of Sorrows Catholic School my primary duties were to open up the building in the morning and to make sure the classrooms were clean and in order. It was also my responsibility to ensure the boiler was running smoothly during the fall and winter. Before the children arrived I would turn on the lights, fire up the boiler and dust mop the hallways. I would take down the chairs in rooms I had damp mopped the day before and pick up any trash left in the schoolyard and parking lot. While classes were in session I would patrol the hallways, dust mop the auditorium, which doubled as a gymnasium, clean the office and library, sweep the stairs and sanitize the restrooms. Once all the children finished lunch I would collect the trash and clean the cafeteria.

When school was done for the day I would prop open the front doors to allow the children to exit in an orderly fashion. The youngest students led by their teachers were always the first to be dismissed. After all the children had vacated the building I would then pick up the chairs and sweep and mop the classrooms for about an hour. Once Sister Patricia and all the teachers had gone home for the day I would turn off the lights, chain up the front doors and make the short walk across the parking lot back to the rectory and get ready for dinner.

It didn't take me long to fall into the daily and weekly cleaning routines. Our Lady of Sorrows parish was located in a predominantly Portuguese neighborhood called Frog Hollow and many of the school children were of Portuguese descent. For lunch I would often run down to the bakery and pick up a fresh roll and drink and relax on the back steps of the rectory to watch the children play during recess. Everybody knew who I was. From here I could see Sister Patricia, the school principal, standing by her office window looking down over the children playing in the parking lot.

I first noticed little Christina, a 4th grader in Miss Avenia's class, acting oddly at recess. She appeared very distant and isolated from the other children. I had seen her several times before walking home from school with her older sister Michelle and a few of her 7th grade friends. Christina always seemed so quiet and reserved, never looking up or speaking to anybody. During recess I found Christina's behavior quite peculiar. Unlike the other children who ran around the parking lot energetically making lots of noise, Christina was unusually quiet and passed her time hidden away all alone in a dark corner. She did have one friend though, another 4th grader named Emily who she would play with occasionally, but Christina never participated in any games or group activities. Sometimes I would see her climbing around on the monkey bars, skipping rope or just swinging in the playground all by herself, but most of the time she just sat around in a corner with her little friend whispering secrets. Every so often I'd catch them peeking over at me or hear them giggling from across the parking lot.

Every day during lunch break I would sit and watch the children play, all the while secretly keeping a close eye on little Christina. One day I looked up and saw her glaring at me from across the parking lot and felt an eerie chill run up my spine. Did she know I was watching her? How long had she been staring at me, and why was I so terrified of a nine or ten year old girl? I think the other children could sense that there was something different about little Christina. I know I sensed it and I'm pretty sure Sister Patricia did too. There was definitely something oddly peculiar and unnerving about her, although I could not quite put my finger on it. Christina's strange behavior made her an outcast, yet somehow she seemed content with that, as if she enjoyed being isolated from the rest of the world.

One day in early December I got called up to Miss Avenia's classroom to change a lightbulb and spotted little Christina seated at her desk drawing in a notebook. Now when I entered the room all the other kids started running around and going wild, but Christina just sat there calmly glaring up at me with a look of contempt and disregard on her face. I suddenly became very nervous and again felt an icy chill run up and down my spine. I hurried up and down the ladder and got out of there as fast as I could.

By mid-December there was already close to a foot of snow on the ground and I found myself having to shovel the sidewalks almost every day just to keep up. *So what time are we closing up shop today, Sister?*

One morning I went into work a couple of hours early and headed straight up to Miss Avenia's 4th grade classroom to have a look around. It was still dark so I switched on the lights and glanced around the room. It only took me a moment to find Christina's desk. It was situated in the front row directly facing the teacher's desk. Christina's desk was very neat and tidy with just a few pencils and erasers on top. Inside was the red notebook with some school papers stuffed in between the pages. Spelled out neatly on the front cover in big, bold letters was her first and last name: Christina Rosario. Curious, I flipped through the notebook to see if she had written anything down, but all the pages were blank except for a few drawings of flowers and butterflies. Apparently Christina was a very smart little girl though because all the school papers were marked 100%, some even had gold stars and stickers on them. It was still dark outside and nobody else was due to arrive for another hour so I closed up Christina's desk, arranged the pencils and erasers just the way I had found them and started in on my usual cleaning routine.

It was Friday, the last day of school before Christmas break and I was just finishing up lunch when I glanced up and noticed

Christina and Emily snickering at me again from across the parking lot. When Christina saw me looking over at them she leaned forward and whispered something into Emily's ear. What happened next was shocking. Out of the blue Emily suddenly came running up to me and said, "My friend wants to know why you keep staring at her?"

I was speechless. Did Christina know I had been spying on her all along? Did she know that I had been snooping around in her desk? This unnerved me and to tell you the truth, I was a little frightened. I gathered my senses and said, "Tell me, what is your friend's name?"

And she replied, "Christina."

"And your name is Emily, correct?" She nodded her head. "Tell me Emily, how come the other kids never talk to Christina?"

"I don't know," she answered. "They just like to stick out their tongues and make fun of her, I guess."

"I see," I said. "Is that why she doesn't play games like the other boys and girls?" Just then the whistle blew signaling the end of recess and she ran off before I could say anything else. As I watched her running away, I glanced up and saw Sister Patricia standing by her window peering down at me with a very concerned look on her face. Had she seen me talking to Emily? I was very nervous and did my best not to cross paths with her for the rest of the day. But nothing ever really became of it. I was after all a part of the school staff now and interacting with the students every now and then was all part of the job...wasn't it?

All throughout Christmas break I thought about little Christina and wondered what it was that made her different than the other children. I mean she looked like any other nine or ten year old catholic girl dressed in her cute little blue and white school uniform and matching PF Flyers. With her long dark hair and big brown eyes she looked just like her older sister and was certainly much prettier than most of the other girls her age. So why did she seem so distant, so secluded, so out of place? I must not let myself become obsessed I thought, but I had to find out what it was that made little Christina so peculiar.

For two weeks I worked my tail off stripping and waxing and polishing the floors. The school was quiet and lonely without the kids around, so I took my portable radio along and listened to the oldies while I worked. Outside I could see the snow piling up on the statue of Mother Mary and the bare, lifeless trees coated with ice.

Michelle Rosario was a bright, friendly, outgoing young lady from Miss Duvall's 7th grade class. She was also very protective of her younger sister. One day after school I decided to follow them home to find out where they lived. Maintaining a safe distance back so I wouldn't be seen, I watched them round the corner and head south down the busy avenue. Following close behind, I took a shortcut through the playground and spotted the two girls just as they turned down a side street about three blocks from the church. From the corner I saw them enter a large white house at 16 Greenwood Road.

Every week the 7th and 8th graders would take turns performing special duties around the school such as straightening up the library, helping out in the office answering the phone when the secretary was out to lunch, or just cleaning up the teacher's lounge. One morning I cornered Michelle in the library as she was restacking books with one of her classmates. "Michelle," I said. "I really need to ask you something in private about your sister. Can you meet me in the basement later on after lunch?"

She looked at me strangely for a moment then said, "You mean Christina?" She seemed puzzled.

"Yes," I answered. She nodded her head and agreed to meet by the boiler room after lunch. The next couple of hours dragged by and with each passing moment I grew more and more anxious as I tried to think of what I would say. By the time the lunch bell finally rung I was a nervous wreck and hid in the boiler room watching for Michelle to come walking down the stairs. But to my surprise it wasn't Michelle who came walking down the stairs at all, it was Sister Patricia and she didn't look very happy.

You can well imagine the shock and dread I felt as I watched her march purposefully down the hallway. "What is the meaning of this?' she demanded. "One of my 7th grade girls came to me this afternoon and she was understandably very upset. She said that you asked her to meet you down here because you were concerned about her younger sister. Would you mind telling me what this is all about please?"

Trying my best to keep my composure, I answered, "I'm sorry, Sister. I didn't mean to cause any trouble, but the other day I noticed Christina acting strangely and thought maybe there was something wrong with her."

Looking me straight in the eye, she said, "I see." She paused for a moment and I braced myself. "I'll look into it," she said. "But from now on if you have any concerns about any of the children, please come directly to me instead of trying to take matters into your own hands. Is that understood?"

"Yes of course, Sister," I answered.

"Good, now please get back to work and for heaven's sake stay away from poor Michelle, she's already been through enough for one day. She is afraid that you might have had bad intentions, and we wouldn't want the children getting the wrong impression now would we?"

"No ma'am," I replied. With that she turned to walk away without another word. As she did, I called out to her and said, "Would you please tell Michelle that I'm really sorry for upsetting her. It won't happen again, I promise." I watched her slowly climb the stairs and disappear from sight.

Now what was I going to do I wondered? Michelle would probably never speak to me again, Sister Patricia will be watching me like a hawk, and to make matters worse, I was still no closer to figuring out what was wrong with little Christina. Was this the beginning of the end for me? Were my days at Our Lady of Sorrows numbered? I was confused and terrified and ashamed of the trouble I had caused. After work I went out for dinner afraid to face Father Joe. By now he would have heard. Later that night as I lay awake in bed expecting Father Joe to come pounding on my door at any moment, I came up with an idea.

One Thursday afternoon in mid-February I was vacuuming

the old worn out carpet in the teacher's lounge when in walks Michelle with one of her classmates. She ignored me when she first entered the room and pretended like I wasn't there, but I could feel her watching me the entire time. When I finished vacuuming I turned around, looked her square in the eye and said, "An occasional 'Hello' would brighten my day."

But she just stared at me blankly and said, "I'm not supposed to talk to you anymore." Suddenly I felt a strange attraction come over me and pictured Michelle in ten or twelve years.

One beautiful spring day in March I was relaxing on the rectory steps after lunch when I noticed little Christina just swinging up and down in the playground all by herself. Could this be the chance I had been waiting for? I looked around to see if anybody was watching me. The 7th and 8th graders were still inside eating lunch so there was no sign of Michelle, and Emily was nowhere to be seen. Sister Patricia was sitting at her desk talking on the phone and Sister Mary Rose, the teacher on recess duty, was occupied with some 1st and 2nd graders playing four-square. I stood up, took a deep breath and strolled casually across the parking lot toward the playground. Christina watched curiously as I neared. When I reached the grass I looked around one more time to make sure nobody else was watching. There were several other children in the playground, but they were too busy horsing around to really notice me, so I crept right up to Christina as she sat swinging gently back and forth and said warily, "Hello Christina...That is your name isn't it?"

Tilting her head slightly to one side, she gazed up at me with those big brown eyes and in a sarcastic tone said, "What do you want?" Her eyes were piercing, her gaze cold and decisive.

"Where is your friend Emily?" I inquired.

"She's not here today," she replied as if she didn't really care. "Emily's not really my friend, I just talk to her sometimes."

"I see. Don't you have any other real friends you can play with?" I asked.

"Nobody likes me," she answered.

"Nobody likes you...? What do you mean nobody likes you?

Why doesn't anybody like you?"

"I don't know," she replied.

"Do you know who I am?" I asked trying to change the subject.

"You're silly!" she giggled mischievously. "Of course I know who you are...You're Mr. Janitor."

"And who are you?" I interjected.

"I already told you before," she countered.

"Well I know your name, but I want to know who you REALLY are?" I demanded.

She paused for a second then calmly leaned forward and half whispering so nobody else could hear, she said, "I am a slimy salamander."

I was stunned. "What did you say?"

"You heard me," she said defiantly. "Now go away and leave me alone!" she ordered. And with that she suddenly jumped down from the swing and went running off. And that was that. I never spoke to little Christina again. I thought about what she had said every day of course, but it wasn't until years later when I was doing research that I fully understood what she meant.

Mozart Woods was a local hangout popular with the older kids in the neighborhood. It was just a small patch of woods really, stretching five or six city blocks with a section of Trout Brook running through the middle of it where the kids would tie a rope and old tire to a tree branch and use as a Tarzan swing to get from one side to the other. The north side of Mozart Woods was only accessible from a dead end street about a mile from Our Lady of Sorrows. The south end was accessible by climbing an old stone wall just yards away from the playground and many of the children used it as a shortcut to get back and forth to and from school. The woods were cool in the summer and were always full of kids riding their mini-bikes along the network of dirt paths. There were still some rusty old 'No Trespassing' signs posted up and down the trail but nobody paid attention to them anymore.

Sometimes early in the morning or evening I would go hiking through the woods just to relax or unwind, following the trail along the brook. Mozart Woods was full of furry critters including possums, raccoons and little brown bats. One particular Saturday evening in mid-April I was walking along the creek at dusk when I heard something rustling in the leaves. I stopped dead in my tracks and stood as still as I could. More stirring up ahead. I slipped my thick leather gloves on and slowly inched forward. I squatted down and started digging cautiously through the debris until I found the source of the noise. Nestled in between an old oak stump and a couple of half-buried boulders was a den of young raccoons. There were five or six of them and they weren't very happy about the intrusion. They couldn't have been more than three or four months old but when they saw me they began to growl and snarl like vicious little demons. Suddenly one of the larger ones came charging out at me all teeth and claws. Instinctively I took a step back and froze. It let out a ferocious growl and lunged up at me so I kicked it aside. The raccoon lunged at me again, but this time I was ready and whacked it on the skull with my flashlight, killing it instantly. The dead raccoon fell limp and lifeless to the ground and I high-tailed out of there as fast as I could. This was one of the worst things I ever had to do in my entire life.

Early the following morning while it was still dark I grabbed my flashlight and a pillow sack and hurried back to the woods to retrieve the dead raccoon. There wouldn't be anybody there at that time of day so I stumbled my way down to the brook where I first found the den. The dead raccoon still lay on the ground undisturbed. No other animals had gotten to it during the night. It still had that horribly vicious, twisted snarl engraved on its frightened face, one I'll never forget as long as I live. The carcass was already starting to decompose a little and there were a few flies around, but it was still fresh and didn't really stink too badly after only twelve hours. The woods were still and silent. Soon it would be daylight so I scooped up the raccoon and slipped it gently into the pillowcase. I carefully carried the lifeless animal over the old stone wall and stashed it in the toolshed behind the church where nobody would find it.

For the most part the other children avoided little Christina during recess, leaving her to play all by herself. However, there were three troublemakers from the 5th and 6th grade who liked to pick on her every chance they could. There was Alex, the lead instigator, whose antics often landed him in the principal's office. Lester was his lanky sidekick who went along with every one of his pranks. Then there was Jimmy Robbins, the chubby 5th grader whose shirt was always untucked who followed them around like a puppy dog everywhere they went. The three boys enjoyed making fun of Christina and I would often see them taunting and teasing her as she swung in the playground. They would stick their tongues out at her, make disgusting faces and call her vulgar names. Most of the time she simply ignored them and after a while they would get bored and give up or get scolded by the teacher and placed in detention.

Following a restless night filled with anxiety and very little sleep, Monday morning I somehow managed to get into work about two hours early. It was Daylight Saving Time and the sun wouldn't be up for another hour and a half. When I got to Our Lady of Sorrows I checked the grounds to make sure there wasn't anybody around. The coast was clear so I unlocked the toolshed, grabbed a shovel, a garden rake and the pillow sack with the dead raccoon stuffed inside and snuck over to the playground behind the school. I took another look around but didn't see any lights on in the rectory. I then dug a shallow hole in the sand just a few yards from the swings. I removed the raccoon from the pillowcase and placed it gently in the hole where I knew the three boys would find it. I covered it up with sand and smoothed out my footprints. I locked up the tools back in the shed and disposed of the smelly pillowcase in the dumpster. I stomped out my feet to shake all the sand from my shoes and dashed into the school. About thirty minutes later I heard the garbage truck come by and empty the dumpster right on schedule.

It was shaping up to be another gorgeous spring day in late April. By noon the clouds had all dissipated and the sunshine warmed temperatures well into the seventies. At recess the children went absolutely wild, running around everywhere with a case of spring fever. Emily was having fun playing games in the parking lot with some of the other 3rd and 4th graders. I glanced up and saw Sister Patricia through her office window, she was sitting at her desk eating lunch. Scanning the schoolyard, I spotted little Christina out of the corner of my eye, she was all alone and heading straight for the playground just as I expected. From my vantage point on the rectory steps I could barely make out the lump in the sand where I had buried the dead raccoon. There were already several kids in the playground when Christina jumped up and started climbing around on the monkey bars. I watched as the three troublemakers followed her into the playground just as I suspected they would. I held my breath in anticipation and fear.

Jimmy Robbins was the first to discover the dead raccoon buried in the sand. In fact, he practically stumbled over it. "Hey Alex....Look what I found!" he said excitedly.

Alex and Lester came running over. "Gross!" I heard one of them say. "Hey I know. Let's scare Christina with it," Lester whispered.

Alex kicked the half-buried raccoon, exposing it even more. Its face was grotesque and contorted. "Hey Christina!" he shouted. "Look at what we found." Christina turned to look and let out a terrifying blood-curdling scream. I stood up to find out what was going on just in time to see her lose her grip and slip from the top of the monkey bars. There was another horrible scream followed by a loud thump as she fell and cracked the back of her head on one of the crossbars and landed flat on her back in the sand unconscious.

Everybody went running toward the playground. The schoolyard was complete chaos and confusion. Kids were gathering around and Miss Avenia had to push her way through. She shouted for someone to call 911. There was screaming and yelling and children crying for help. By this time Sister Patricia and the other teachers heard all the commotion and came rushing out to see what was happening. Dolores, the church secretary, saw the utter chaos from her office window and immediately called 911. As more and more children continued pouring into the parking lot, including Michelle and most of her 7th grade classmates, Sister Patricia and the other teachers blew their whistles and shouted at them to get back as they tried frantically to keep the children away from the playground. I heard sirens in the distance.

By this time Father Joe had also come out to try and help restore order. Sister Patricia and the other teachers were finally able to corral most of the children back inside, but Michelle was still left standing over by the playground. Her hands were covering her face and she was sobbing hysterically. Miss Duvall saw her and went running over. She put her arm around the poor frightened teenager and did her best to comfort and console her as she escorted her back into the school. Sister Patricia tried to keep everybody calm as Father Joe knelt down and cradled Christina's head, but there was blood coming from her mouth and she wasn't breathing. Miss Avenia attempted to resuscitate the little girl, but she was already gone and everybody knew it.

Moments later the police and paramedics arrived and we all stood around watching and praying nervously as they tried desperately to save her. But it was already too late. She had died instantaneously from the impact. The schoolyard was deathly silent as the paramedics tried over and over to breathe life into the young girl, but it was just no use and they finally had to give up and covered her up with a blanket. Little Christina was pronounced dead at the scene. Christina's tragic death on the playground that day was ruled a horrible accident.

News spread quickly through the community and everybody was in shock and mourning. School closed for the rest of the week as the town grieved and did its best to cope with the terrible tragedy. Sister Patricia and I were the only ones there for the next several days. I knew that she blamed me for Christina's death and on Wednesday she confronted me while I was dust mopping the hallway as I knew she eventually would. "Do you know anything about what happened out there?" I flatly denied knowing anything at all about it. Now it should be said that I am not in the habit of lying to anybody, particularly nuns or priests, but under the circumstances I felt it was probably the smart thing to do. On Thursday inspectors from the local Archdiocese Office came out to have a look around and declared the playground unsafe to use. The playground was shut down for the remainder of the school year and the children were ordered to keep out until further notice.

On Monday the school reopened and things slowly got back to normal, but Michelle was not there. Neither was Alex or Lester. I heard through the grapevine that they had been suspended from Our Lady of Sorrows indefinitely. At recess the children sullenly played games in the parking lot and stayed away from the condemned playground as they were told. The fence dividing the grassy area from the playground had been miraculously transformed into a makeshift memorial for little Christina. By the end of the week it was fully decorated with flowers, stuffed animals and red butterfly balloons. There were also crosses lining the fence and lots of cards and notes which the children had written to honor and remember her by. Two teachers were now assigned to recess duty for the rest of the school year instead of just one. By Thursday I noticed that Michelle still had not returned to school. Understandable I guess given the circumstances. A dark cloud hung over Our Lady of Sorrows for weeks.

On Friday morning all the students and staff from Our Lady of Sorrows along with hundreds of anguished parishioners and others from the community crowded into the church to attend Christina's funeral and say their final goodbyes. Consumed by guilt, I couldn't bring myself to go so I stayed behind. While everybody was away I went into Miss Avenia's 4th grade classroom to take another look around. Christina's desk still stood where it always had in the front of the room. It too had been turned into a makeshift memorial beautifully adorned with flowers and cards from her classmates. I slowly opened it up to have a peek. Christina's red notebook was still inside stuffed with old school papers just the way I remembered. But what I found next shocked me beyond belief. Underneath the notebook was a map of the United States with the state of Arkansas circled in red magic marker and a picture of a hellbender salamander that she must have cut out of a magazine and glued to the map. I was sure it was meant for me, but what did it mean? I slammed the desk shut, replaced the flowers and cards the way I had found them and left the room.

Later that day little Christina Rosario's body was buried in Mount Saint Francis Catholic Cemetery just on the other side of town. Michelle Rosario never returned to Our Lady of Sorrows. One day I walked down to Greenwood Road past the big white house where I had once seen the two girls go after school and noticed a 'For Sale' sign in the front yard. Michelle and her widowed mother had moved out. The next day I took an envelope and wrote Michelle's name and address on it along with my return address at the boarding house. I folded up a blank piece of paper, stuffed it in the envelope like a letter and dropped it in the mailbox on the corner. The following week the envelope came back stamped 'Return to Sender'. I rushed down to the Post Office to see if I could get a forwarding address, but the clerk said there was no forwarding address available for the Rosarios who used to live at 16 Greenwood Road.

One Saturday afternoon in mid-May after things had finally settled down at the school, I made the fifteen minute bus ride across town to visit Christina's gravesite. Mount Saint Francis Cemetery sat on a large parcel of land roughly a hundred and fifty acres on the outskirts of town not far from the county line. When I got to the cemetery I checked the map to see if Christina's plot was listed, but I couldn't find it so I searched the grounds until I finally located her grave. It was in a shady section toward the back of the cemetery surrounded by trees and statues of weeping angels. A bouquet of flowers that somebody had left just days before lay wilting on the grass. Could it have been Michelle and her mother I wondered?

I crouched down to read the headstone. Little Christina was only ten years old when she died. So sad. When I looked closer I noticed fresh claw marks on the ground that had been made by some kind of animal digging around her grave. I was shocked by this and checked the area, but none of the other graves appeared to have been disturbed. It was almost dusk and they would be closing the cemetery soon so I headed down the path toward the gate to catch my bus home when I suddenly got the strangest feeling that somebody or something was watching me. I stopped and looked around, but the cemetery was completely empty so I high-tailed out of there as fast as I could. When I got back into town I stopped at a phone booth a few blocks from home and in the directory I found a number listed for a Rosario on Greenwood Road. I dropped a quarter in the slot and dialed, but the number of course had been disconnected.

SALAMANDER SPRINGS

For three days and three nights the two men hiked across the rugged Ozark Mountains up and down trails with names like Eagle Crest, Jagged Rock and Wolf Creek. They trekked north through the wilderness winding past creeks, cascading waterfalls, bluffs and crags in the shapes of animal heads. They were strangers and didn't talk much. Laughing Crow, as he liked to be called, was a young Choctaw Indian from a settlement just outside of Conway. Charlie had made the forty hour bus ride from New York and hired the young scout for $100 a day to guide him to a place called Salamander Springs, about thirty miles from the Arkansas/Missouri state line. At night they set up camp and took turns sleeping for three or four hours while the other kept watch with a high-powered rifle loaded with enough buckshot to take down a grizzly bear. Charlie took the first watch. At around midnight Charlie would wake up the Indian guide to take the graveyard shift and guard the camp as he rested. At sunup the two men would pack up their gear and resume their trek through the forest.

The first day it poured down rain the entire time and they didn't see a thing. The rain continued into the evening and by nightfall both men were drenched, exhausted and hungry, so they pitched their tents under a canopy of tall cedars and sycamores.

The second day started off foggy, but by mid-morning the sun came out making the journey much more pleasant. At around noon Charlie and the Indian guide stopped to rest at Fish Creek and had a bite to eat. Nearby there was an old abandoned campsite that looked like it hadn't been occupied in years. After lunch they crossed an old footbridge over the creek and were greeted on the other side by a beautiful meadow covered in wildflowers and a beaver pond the size of a small lake. They passed through an old limestone cavern full of brown bats roosting in the cracks between the rocks. The cave was dark, damp and cool with a subterranean hot springs. They hiked almost twenty miles that day and observed plenty of wildlife along the way including some elk, a couple of badgers, and a rattlesnake that happened to cross their path, which could have proven disastrous had they taken the horses along. At night the forest came alive with the sounds of screech owls and croaking frogs. They could even hear wolves or coyotes howling in the distance.

The next morning Charlie and Laughing Crow woke up refreshed and ready to go, anxious to reach their destination. "Salamander Springs is only another ten miles or so," the Indian reassured Charlie. "We should be there in a couple of hours."

Salamanders Springs was a remote densely forested area deep in the Ozarks surrounded by huge moss-covered boulders, flatrocks and plateaus. The panoramic view of the mountains from the hillside overlooking the creek was absolutely breathtaking. They set up camp in a clearing a few hundred yards from the trail. "How many times have you been up here?" Charlie asked.

"Many times," the Indian said.

"Ever see anything unusual?"

"Like what?" the Indian inquired.

"Oh I don't know, anything strange or out of the ordinary. How about other hikers or campers? Ever see any of them up here hunting or fishing or anything like that?"

"Not that I recall. There aren't any roads leading in and out of here and it's a long, treacherous hike as you know." The Choctaw pointed to the east and said, "The nearest town is ten miles away and I ain't never seen any park rangers patrolling these woods either. There is an old Indian burial ground not far from here though. I have heard stories about some ghosts and spirits that supposedly haunt these woods at night."

"Really?" Charlie said curiously. "Can you take me there?"

"No I'm afraid not. I am forbidden by my elders to even go there myself."

"But you've been there before right?" Charlie implored. "I mean you know where it is don't you?"

"Not exactly. It was a long time ago."

"Do you have any ancestors buried there?" Charlie said.

"A few." the Indian paused for a moment and said, "Tell me, why did you really hire me to bring you up to Salamander Springs? It wasn't to admire the scenery or photograph the animals, you could have done that anywhere."

Knowing that what he was about to say was only half the truth, and half the story, Charlie replied, "Actually yes. I read somewhere that there is supposed to be a population of hellbender salamanders living in the creek. I hired you to take me up here so I could photograph them."

"You mean to tell me that you hired me to bring you all the way out here just so you could take pictures of these salamanders you read about in some brochure?"

"Yup. Have you ever seen any around here?"

"No, I can't say that I have," the Indian said. "But I have seen them down in some of the other creeks."

"And what about those ghosts and spirits you mentioned? Ever see any of them roaming around here?" Charlie asked.

True to his name, Laughing Crow chuckled and said, "No I can't say that I have, but you know a large animal moving around in the woods at night could easily be mistaken for a ghost or a spirit."

"You're probably right. Well let's say we go down to the creek and see if we can't find some of them salamanders. What do you say?"

"Sure why not, we still have a couple of hours of daylight. What the hell are we waiting for? Let's go!" Both men chuckled some more and headed down the embankment.

When they got down to the creek the two men took off their

boots and socks, rolled up their pant legs and waded into the cold water until it was rushing and swirling up past their knees. "The little ones have bushy gills and the adults are big and ugly with wrinkly skin and small black eyes," Charlie said as they started overturning rocks, some of them so heavy that it took both men just to pry them loose from the sediment. Almost half an hour past and they still hadn't seen a single salamander. But then as they lifted up this one huge flatrock, a giant hellbender suddenly came darting out. Charlie chased it downstream but lost it in the swift current. Both men searched for it again and finally found it hiding in a rift near the streambank.

"Look at the size of that thing," the Indian said. Charlie lunged for the salamander and snagged it with his fishnet before it could swim away. It was a two foot long monster. It was slippery and slimy and fighting desperately to escape. It managed to get away when Charlie tried to untangle it from the net and the giant amphibian jumped back into the water with a loud splash. They spotted another one crawling around on the bottom of the creek a few moments later, but it got away before they could catch it. By now it was getting close to dusk so the two men hiked back to camp to fix dinner and sack out for the night.

Just a stone's throw away from the field where the two men had set up camp was a bluff with a steep hundred foot vertical drop into a rocky ravine. Charlie and Laughing Crow sat on the grass looking out over the bluff where they could watch the sunset and shared a bottle of Kentucky moonshine. The view of the Ozarks was spectacular and as they passed the bottle of Old Crow back and forth, the Choctaw Indian told Charlie stories that he had heard from one of the elders in his tribe.

It was almost dusk when Charlie stood up and stumbled clumsily into the woods to take a leak. When he got back the Indian was on his feet with his rifle cocked and ready. "What is it....Did you see something?" Charlie asked.

"Ssshhh!" the Indian motioned for him to stand still. "Look over there....Do you see them?" He pointed toward the bluff.

Charlie squinted his eyes in the fading light but didn't see anything at first until one of them moved. "Oh my God....What the hell is that?" he said. They started creeping toward the two men from both sides of the field. "What the hell are those?" Charlie asked again.

"Don't move," the Indian said. Both men stood motionless.

"Are those fuckin' wolves?" Charlie implored. The animals slowly inched forward and began forming a circle around them.

"Them ain't wolves, Charlie....Those are red foxes and it looks like they're getting ready to pounce."

"Foxes? This is fuckin' crazy!" Charlie counted them instinctively. There were thirteen of them. "Wait a minute....foxes don't usually hunt in packs. Why the hell are they stalking us like that?" Charlie could see their eyes glowing in the twilight as they closed in on the men and surrounded them.

"I don't know but I'm not about to wait around and find out." Laughing Crow raised his rifle and fired off a warning shot. The gunshot pierced the night, echoing through the canyon below. The loud blast startled the pack and they scattered in all directions. But a moment later the foxes came at them again and encircled the frightened men. The Indian fired his rifle into the air a second time. This time the terrified foxes ran away and bolted over the side of the cliff one right after another, howling and whining horrendously as they plunged to their death. That is, all but one which just stood there unafraid watching them from across the field. Suddenly the fox raised its head, let out a chilling howl and started to creep forward.

"That's no ordinary fox. What the hell is that thing?" the Indian said.

"I don't know, but the damn thing looks possessed! Kill it!" Charlie shouted and the creature charged. The Choctaw aimed his rifle and fired off another round. But his hands were shaking so badly that the bullet missed its mark and whizzed by the creature. The Indian cocked his rifle again. But before he could get another shot off, the creature let out a terrifying cry then turned and vaulted over the edge and plummeted into the ravine. The two men ran across the field and peered over the edge. The ravine was pitch black and they could barely make out the silhouettes of the dead foxes strewn about in the rocks at the bottom. They stood up and froze in place. What started as a soft, low-pitched buzzing sound gradually grew higher and higher and louder and louder, increasing in pitch and in volume until it reached a crescendo so intense that it sounded like a wailing siren and both men had to cover their ears. "Now what the hell is that?" Charlie shouted, but the Indian couldn't hear a word he was saying. They both took a step back and turned to run when all of a sudden a red-tailed hawk shot straight up from the bottom of the ravine with a deafening screech. The two stunned men watched in utter awe as the raptor accelerated like a missile, ascending higher and higher into the air and slowly disappeared into the starry sky. Everything was silent and still again.

Finally the Choctaw said, "What the hell just happened?"

"I don't know, but we gotta get the fuck outa here. How far did you say that town was again?"

"Badger? About ten miles. But we can't hike out of here now, we'll have to wait until morning," the Indian said.

"You're right. Well, I suggest we try to get some rest until then."

At the crack of dawn Charlie and Laughing Crow packed up their gear and hiked out of Salamander Springs. They parted ways in Badger, vowing to stay in touch. Charlie hitchhiked into Fayetteville to catch a Greyhound while the Indian called for somebody to come pick him up and take him back to Conway. Both men swore that they would never speak a word to anyone about their bizarre experience that day at Salamander Springs.

GIRL ON THE #9 BUS

Preface

Monsters really do exist, of that I am certain. Now I'm not talking about vampires, werewolves or zombies, or the kind that hide in your closet or under your bed. No sir. I'm talking about monsters that can disguise themselves in any form they choose and blend in so well you won't even know they're there. But these monsters aren't out to kill and destroy. Oh no, they're too clever for that. They would much rather play games and always seem to know what your next move will be, should you challenge them. These are creatures of superior intelligence with the cunning of serpents, and the ability to camouflage themselves like chameleons. They are as elusive as butterflies, slippier than eels, and will stalk you like a leopard in the dark. They will shadow you during the day and haunt your dreams at night. They will leave a trail of breadcrumbs for you to follow, then lure you into their traps just for amusement. They are playful and will make you do awful things as you attempt to expose them.

I will never forget the day I first saw Amanda on the #9 bus. I overslept and had to scramble around just to catch the bus in time for work. Outside it was pouring down rain and it was foggy. I ran across the street and made it to the bus stop just as the 8 o'clock bus was pulling up to the curb. It was jam packed with college students and people commuting to work. There was barely enough room to breathe.

I managed to find an empty seat by the window about halfway

down the aisle. A spiffy looking businessman carrying a briefcase sat down beside me and nodded politely. In the seat in front of him there was an elderly woman with a walker that was partially blocking the aisle. And seated by the window directly in front of me I noticed an attractive young girl with long dark hair. She wore tight fitting jeans, a long raincoat, and knee high boots. She was probably in her early twenties and most likely a college student. I recognized most of the people on the bus as regular passengers, but I couldn't recall ever seeing her before, and I'm sure I would have noticed.

Inside the bus the windows were all steamed up, so I cleared a spot with my sleeve where I could look out at the buildings passing by. The businessman started to cough and fidget, so I pulled out my paperback and pretended to read. Five minutes later the bus pulled up in front of the college. The girl in front of me stood up and nudged her way toward the rear exit. She was exceptionally pretty. She must have sensed I was staring because she flashed me a friendly smile as she went by. Knowing I'd been caught, I turned around to look out the window when I noticed something written on the glass right by the spot I had cleared. It read: "*Hi Billy.*" Billy is my name, but I certainly didn't write it, and I think I would have seen whoever did because I never left my seat. I was puzzled, intrigued and a little bit disturbed. It was then I realized that it must have been the college girl. Somehow she must have scrawled my name on the glass with her finger when I wasn't paying attention. But how was that even possible? I would have seen her. I looked out the window to see if I could spot her and there she was just standing there under her umbrella smiling up at me.

I jerked back instinctively as the bus pulled away. The businessman gave me a dirty look and moved to another seat. I was really uneasy and didn't know what to do. Should I get off the bus and confront her, or just continue on my way and pretend like nothing happened? I casually wiped the writing off the window, waited until the bus stopped a few blocks from the college, and hopped off. I hurried back up the hill through the pouring rain and hid in the small cafe across the street. Visibly shaken and soaking wet, I ordered a cup of coffee and sat down on a stool by the window. There was a group of college kids hanging around outside, but by this time most of the students were already in class. I sat there for about a half an hour, nervously sipping my coffee just hoping that I might catch another glimpse of the mysterious girl from the bus. I was already late for work so I called my boss to tell him I wouldn't be coming in. I gathered up my things, left the cafe, and walked to the corner to catch the bus home.

I had the following day off, but I caught the 8 o'clock bus going downtown anyway. It wasn't nearly as packed as it was the previous day and this time I found an empty seat in the rear of the bus. As I walked down the aisle I spotted the mysterious college girl in the corner of my eye. She was sitting all alone in the middle of the bus. She glanced up and smiled coquettishly as I passed by, which gave me a chill. We again made eye contact and my heart started pounding faster. She was absolutely breathtaking. I finally reached the back of the bus and sat down nervously. A few minutes later the bus pulled up in front of the college and the kids started filing off. The mysterious girl stood up, paused a moment, then looked directly at me and smiled again, as if she knew exactly where I'd be sitting. When I peered out the window to see which way she was going, she suddenly turned around and waved at me just as the bus drove away.

I immediately rang the buzzer to signal I wanted off at the next stop. I trotted back up the hill to the college. This time there were lots of kids milling around, but the mysterious girl was nowhere to be seen. I dashed across the street and ducked into the cafe for another cup of coffee. I sat down and just stared out the window for about twenty minutes, but still didn't see any sign of her. It was as though she had simply vanished into thin air. I was just about ready to give up when a couple of college kids came walking in. I recognized them right away from the bus. I waited until they got their drinks and sat down. They started joking around with each other and kept glancing over in my direction. I finished the last of my coffee and got up to leave. As I walked by their table one of them turned to me and said, "What's up, dude? Hey, you ride that dreaded morning bus too, don't you?"

"Oh yeah, I see you guys on there all the time. What's going on?" I asked.

"Nothing much really," the other one said. "Just grabbing some coffee before class. What're you on your way to work or something?"

"No, not today," I answered. "It's my day off. Say, maybe you guys can help me out…?" I inquired. "I thought I recognized somebody on the bus this morning. Maybe you guys know who she is?"

"I don't know, dude. Who is she?" the first one said and they both started to chuckle.

"I don't know her name or nothing, but she has long brown hair and was sitting in the middle of the bus," I explained.

They looked at each other and thought about it for a moment. "I don't know, bro. Could be Becky, but she don't ride the bus much anymore. Where did you say you knew her from again?" he asked suspiciously.

"She used to be an old neighbor of mine," I lied. "I think she lived a few houses down from me."

Just then the other kid interrupted, "You mean that weird sophomore chick that always rides the bus by herself? What's her name, Amanda or something?"

"Oh yeah, her!" his friend confirmed. "She's definitely a strange one. I don't think she has any friends."

"Well listen, man," the second one said. "We really gotta get going or we'll be late for class. It was sure nice talking to you, and good luck."

"See you later," the other one said and they got up to leave.

"Thanks guys. See you around."

Amanda huh? I had a difficult time getting to sleep that night, but Saturday morning I woke up refreshed and ready to take on the day. I wondered if the mysterious college girl lived close by. She didn't look familiar and her name didn't ring a bell, yet somehow she knew who I was. How else could she have known my name? I wondered what else she knew about me.

I called my mom to tell her I'd be dropping by after lunch and left the apartment. It was a pleasant day for a change, so I caught an uptown bus to the mall and strolled about the shops for a while, just to see if the mysterious college girl happened to be out and about. I wandered the streets for a good hour or more, but still didn't see her around anywhere. So I stopped in one of my favorite restaurants for a bite to eat then hopped a crosstown bus to drop by on my mother for a short visit. It had been a few weeks since I had seen her.

When I arrived at my old house, my mother greeted me with a big hug and we sat down and chatted over a fresh pot of coffee. We talked about the usual stuff - My work, my social life, and that sort of thing. As I was getting ready to go, my mom asked if I had a new girlfriend. I told her that I didn't, and she said, "That's funny. Are you sure? Because a very polite young lady by the name of Amanda called just before you got here and asked me if you were on your way. She sounded very sweet."

I tried my hardest to stay calm and pretend as if I had never heard of her before. "Did you tell her I was on my way over?" I asked.

"Yes of course. She said she'd call you later. Is everything alright, dear" You seem troubled."

"Yes, mom. Everything is fine," I reassured her.

"She sounded quite young, Billy. How old is this new girlfriend of yours anyway?"

"I don't know, mom. I told you, she's not my girlfriend. I better be going now. I'll call you in a couple of days, OK?"

"Sure, honey." She gave me a big hug and kiss and I rushed out the door, anxious to get home before Amanda called.

When I got back to the apartment, I noticed that somebody had called and left a message. I turned on the answering machine. The voice on the recording sounded creepy and slightly distorted. It was that of a young girl and this is what she said: "Hello, Billy. This is your new girlfriend, Amanda. Sorry we missed each other at the mall today. But don't worry, I'll be there waiting for you tomorrow. See you then." I heard childish laughter, followed by a busy signal and a dial tone, then the phone went dead. I checked the caller ID but the number was unavailable. I yanked the cord from the wall in frustration and fell back in my easy chair. How the hell did she know I was at the mall too? She must have followed me from the moment I left my apartment. For all I knew she was still watching me. I slowly walked over to the window, parted the curtains, and looked down over the busy intersection. Could she be hiding in plain sight? I was growing weary of this game of cat-and-mouse. In fact, I wasn't even sure who the cat and who the mouse was anymore.

On Sunday morning, I hopped the uptown bus and got to the mall just as they were opening the doors. There was a line of shoppers waiting to get in. I took the escalator to the upper level and found an empty table in the food court where I could sit down and drink my coffee. I watched the people coming and going as I waited nervously for Amanda to find me. I carefully scanned the pavilion to see if I could spot her spying on me and catch her at her own game.

Almost an hour passed and I still didn't see any sign of Amanda. I started to wonder if I had been stood up. I opened my paperback and began reading. A few minutes had hardly gone by when I heard the click-clack of boot heels approaching from behind. I spun around in my chair and there she stood just smiling down at me seductively. I was stunned. She was easily the most beautiful girl I had ever laid eyes on. She wore skinny jeans, a tight tee shirt, and her raincoat was unbuttoned, revealing a full, curvy, voluptuous figure. Her legs were long and slender. "Mind if I sit down?" she asked in a soft sultry voice.

"No of course not. Please do," I said, gesturing to the chair across from me. I was completely mesmerized by her charms. Her long chestnut colored hair was silky and smooth. She wore a pair of dazzling diamond studded earrings, and her deep blue eyes were positively dreamy. They were the color of midnight, and they seemed to pull me in as if I were falling under some kind of seductive spell.

"Like what you see, Billy?" She said flirtatiously. "You know, if you play your cards right, you might get to see even more of me later." I was speechless. "What's the matter, cat got your tongue?"

She held my gaze with those big hypnotic eyes. I tried to look away, but I simply could not take my eyes off of her. Finally I said, "What do you want from me? I mean, why are you so interested in me. I don't even know you."

"Oh, but I think you do. After all, I know you, don't I, Billy?" she said sarcastically.

I was dumbfounded. "How do you know my name?"

"That was easy," she replied.

"Why have you been following me around? You don't know anything about me."

She leaned forward and said with a mysterious smile, "Oh, but that's where you're wrong, Billy. I know *everything* about you."

"Oh yeah? Like what? We've never even met before."

"I know you like pretty girls."

"How the hell did you get my mother's number anyway?" I demanded to know.

"The same way I got yours. In the phonebook, of course," she said nonchalantly.

"What do you want from me?" I asked again. "You have no business following me around. Don't you have a boyfriend?"

"Why are you interested?" She paused for a second. "We could go out on a date sometime. I'll bet you'd like that, wouldn't you, Billy?"

"I wanna know why you are so interested in me?"

"It's really quite simple," she said biting down on her lip. "I've always found men to be shallow, ignorant little twits. They are dull, self-centered and usually quite obnoxious. But you, Billy, are the exact opposite. You are extremely intelligent, very inquisitive, and you have a certain air of confidence about you which I find irresistibly attractive."

"I'm flattered, really I am. I'm just not used to being stalked by pretty girls. I'm sure you understand," I said.

With that, she stood up unexpectedly and said, "I'm sorry. You'll have to excuse me, but I really must be going now." She reached into her handbag, pulled out an envelope, and set it down on the table in front of me. "I sure hope you'll come by to see more of me later. I'll be waiting for you. You won't be disappointed, I promise." She flashed one last provocative smile before turning to leave, I watched her casually walk away.

I immediately tore open the envelope, nearly ripping the letter inside. I unfolded the letter and read the address: 444 Devereux Hill Drive. I knew the area well. Devereux Hill was located in Cardinal Crest, right off Davenport Road on the outskirts of town, roughly twenty miles from the mall. I stuffed the letter in my pocket and looked around. It was only 11:15 and the food court was already packed with hungry shoppers. Now it was my turn to follow her for a change. I stood up abruptly, nearly tipping over my chair, and bolted across the crowded pavilion. I was only thirty seconds behind her. Everybody turned to gawk in astonishment as I practically flew down the escalator and sprinted through the lobby toward the exit. I pushed hard on the door and stepped outside to see if I could spot her, but once again she had simply vanished. It was then I noticed a couple of security guards eyeing me suspiciously, so I lit a cigarette and walked leisurely back to the bus stop.

When I got back to the apartment I called my mother to ask her if I could borrow the car for a few hours. I told her I had a date with a cute girl from the college. She asked if it was the same one who called looking for me the other day. I explained that it wasn't and said her name was Becky, or Brenda, or something, and that we just met at the mall. She readily agreed.

When I arrived at my mom's place around 6 o'clock, she was waiting for me on the front porch. She handed me the keys and said, "Have a good time, dear! Drive safe and have the car back by midnight please." The old Ford wagon fired right up, so I drove into town and filled up the tank just in case. I took the main drag out of town and turned left onto Davenport Road heading east toward Cardinal Crest. I drove by farmhouses, rolling pastures, dense woods, and miles and miles of cornfields. By the time I got to Devereux Hill it was already getting dark, but the old Fairmont climbed the steep incline with ease. I cruised past the Historical Society and the old cemetery. From the top of the hill, I could barely make out the dark silhouettes of the headstones and museum looming in the headlights.

Her house was at the top of Devereux Hill. I did a quick drive by of the place. It was a large, two story Victorian brownstone mansion. The house was dark and mysterious, except for a single light that shone through from one of the second story windows. I switched off my headlights, pulled into the church parking lot about a half mile away, and shut off the engine. I locked the wagon, pocketed the keys, and hiked back up the hill toward the house.

The old iron gates leading down the long driveway were wide open, so I stopped to take a good look around. I've always had a morbid fascination for the macabre, but this place was downright spooky. It literally gave me goosebumps. I felt uneasy and apprehensive, and wondered if I should go through with it or not. I even considered just turning around and going back home, but in the end my infatuation for Amanda got the better of me. I pulled the hoodie up over my head and started creeping cautiously down the driveway.

Everything was silent and still except for the old weather vane and the giant oak trees creaking in the wind, and the occasional passing car. The front lawn was scraggly and looked as though it hadn't been mowed in months. There was an old forgotten flower garden with a rundown gazebo that was in need of a fresh coat of paint. When I finally reached the steps leading up to the front porch, I was greeted by a pair of giant stone griffins staring down at me with menacing expressions. The big front door was constructed of thick heavy wood and the red paint was chipped and faded. There was a brass lion's head door knocker which looked as though it had recently been polished. I decided I better have a look around out back before I announced my arrival, just to make sure there were no hidden dangers lurking in the shadows. There were more oak trees and the tall grass was overrun with daisies and violets. I could hear the sound of wind chimes tinkling gently in the breeze. Over beyond the embankment, near the edge of the property, by a dense patch of woods, I noticed what appeared to be an old dilapidated servants' quarters covered with ivy. And in the middle of the lawn stood an old bronze sundial with the life-sized statue of a raven perched precariously on the tip of the pointer.

 I snuck around to the back of the house and slithered up the other side until I again found myself face to face with the winged griffins. But this time the front door was propped wide open, as if somebody were trying to entice me inside. I slowly crept up the crumbling concrete steps and hesitated. Inside, the house was pitch black and silent. Taking a deep breath, I crossed the threshold and entered the gloomy mansion. It smelled damp and musty. I gradually inched forward into the darkness, the floorboards creaking and cracking under my weight. Without warning a violent gust of wind came swirling out of nowhere and whipped through the vestibule, slamming the big front door shut with a loud thump. Startled, I jumped back with fright and stumbled into something very large and heavy. It was an antique grandfather clock. But it wasn't just any old grandfather clock, it was the same one my grandparents owned before they passed away. I recognized it from my childhood when we would go and visit them at the farm up on Bluebird Lane. This was no coincidence. Every detail was exactly the way I remembered from the clockmaker's signature to the patterns on the wood. To the familiar rhythmic ticking sound the pendulum made as it swung back and forth, right down to the scratches in the walnut, the chip in the crown, and the cracked faceplate from the time I accidentally tipped it over when I was just nine or ten. I stretched out a hand to steady the swaying timepiece before it could come crashing down on top of me.

 I found a light switch on the wall and flipped it on. A chandelier lit up, dimly illuminating the room in a pale glow. At the far end of the hallway was a parlor with a long flight of stairs twisting its way up past the balcony to the second floor. On one side of the staircase was a beautiful old Steinway, and on the other side a magnificent marble labyrinth. I fumbled over to the foot of the stairs and hollered. "Hello...Is anybody home? Amanda, are you up there? It's me, Billy..." Nothing. The house was perfectly still. I called out her name again, "Are you here, Amanda? It's me, Billy. I know you're up there."

Not a sound, just the tick-tock of the old grandfather clock. I had just about enough of her charades. I was determined to put an end to this game of hide-n-seek once and for all and charged up the stairs. The second floor was dark too, except for a faint flickering shaft of light leaking out from under the crack of one of the doors at the end of the long hallway. I crept quietly down the hall. I leaned forward, put my ear against the door and listened. Soft music was playing inside the room. It sounded scratchy like an old phonograph record. I knocked on the door and called her name one more time, "Amanda, open up. I know you're in there." I tried turning the doorknob, but the room was locked. Suddenly the music stopped playing and the room was eerily quiet. "Amanda, are you in there? Open the door!" I shouted.

Then I heard her soft sultry voice whisper and say, "Welcome, Billy. Won't you come in?" I rattled the handle again, but the door wouldn't budge. Now my blood was really pumping. Exasperated, I slammed into the door with all my weight, splintering the frame to pieces. The door flung open, spilling shards of light into the narrow hall, and I burst into the room...

The two college kids boarded the #9 bus at 7:55AM. As usual, it was packed full of commuters on their way to work, but they managed to find a couple of seats in the back of the bus. "Hey, dude, check it out," one said, gesturing toward the middle seats. "There's that weird chick from English Lit. You know, the one that dude at the coffee shop was talking about."

"Oh yeah. I ain't seen her in a while. I wonder where she's been hiding lately," the other one said.

"I don't know, man, but she sure is smokin' hot!"

"No kidding. Come to think of it, I ain't seen that dude around lately either."

"Maybe he got a new job or something," the first one surmised.

"Yeah, you're probably right." He paused for a second then said, "Hey, speaking of smokin' hot, did you hear about that big fire up on Devereux Hill over the weekend?" he asked.

"Yup, I saw something about it last night on the news," the first one confirmed.

"I guess one of them spooky old haunted mansions by the museum went up in flames in the middle of the night. Evidently they pulled some guy out alive just before it burned to the ground. They said it started in one of the upstairs bedrooms or something. Oh, and get this. They think it might have been intentionally set."

MADALYNE VANDEVEER

On the west side of London where the wealthy and well-to-do gather in the coffee shops and in the opium dens, there was a brothel over in Rosemont on Cranston Street by the name of Bardow Parlors. Bardow Parlors was a high-class bordello run by Madame Dupree which catered exclusively to aristocrats and dignitaries. The courtesans working there were young, beautiful and expensive. Of the dozen or so strumpets who offered their services at Bardow Parlors, there was one exceptionally bodacious tart by the name of Madalyne who was so popular among Madame Dupree's clientele that she even had her own private penthouse which only the richest of the rich could afford to visit. Madalyne was of Flemish descent and looked exquisitely charming and foxy, with long auburn hair and big blue eyes resembling those of a Siamese cat. The lady's soft, supple skin was perfectly flawless and silky smooth to the touch. Her flowery scent was sweet and intoxicating like apple blossoms. Unlike the other prostitutes at the brothel who donned gaudy colorful hats and long flowing skirts, Madalyne always wore her hair down and dressed scantily in slinky scarlet and purple skirts, sashes and scarves with roses, magnolias and lilies embroidered in fine silk. Everyday Madalyne would sit at her vanity methodically brushing her long silky hair and gaze at her reflection in the looking glass, saying to herself with pride, "I am so beautiful. Every man desires me."

Sir Francis Draconian was the only son of a wealthy sea

merchant who made his fortune sailing the seven seas selling and trading silk, furs, spices and many other valuable commodities throughout London and beyond. Sir Francis inherited the noble Draconian estate and all his father's wealth at the age of eighteen and carried on the tradition as a hardworking maritime entrepreneur. He had a reputation as a savvy businessman who dealt only with the upper echelon in Europe, Asia and Africa. Sir Francis Draconian was also very fond of Madalyne and on Friday and Saturday evenings he would take his chauffeur and two of his finest thoroughbreds and ride to Rosemont on Cranston Street to spend the night in her penthouse suite. Whenever he came calling on Madalyne he always showered her with exotic gifts and treasures from around the world to enhance her lavish and luxurious lifestyle. He presented her with dazzling jewelry, jade and cinnabar from the Far East; ivory, wedgewood, crystal balls, and shiny mirrors, as well as a rare collection of miniature intricately painted figureheads carved from the finest ebony, rosewood and aquilaria. He brought her sweetly fragranced incense and candles, perfumes and scented bath oils from France; sumptuous shawls and furs of mink, sable and fox, magnificent sculptures and paintings by the Masters from Spain and Italy; bronze and marble statues, vessels of silver and gold encrusted with precious stones, and alabaster from the north of Africa. And of course Madalyne's favorite piece, a stunning 18k gold salamander brooch from 15th century France which she wore wherever she went. The stickpin was beautifully engraved in delicate detail. The back was set with a line of alternating mother of pearls and Persian turquoise cabochon, the eyes set with two large radiant emeralds from Egypt.

    Sir Francis' infatuation for this beautiful young harlot became an obsession and he soon found himself falling hopelessly in love. Sometimes he would take her out to the theater where they would put on quite a show themselves. She would then escort him to a fancy restaurant by the wharf or go on a long carriage ride along the Thames before returning to her penthouse for the night. Out in public Madalyne's sultry, skimpy outfits often caused quite a stir, but she was really a perfect gentleman's lady. In bed the baron could always count on her to be a real nymphomaniac, experimenting with sexual pleasures and fetishes he had only dreamed of in his youth. Naturally all the other bawds at Madame Dupree's brothel were jealous of Madalyne and they would lash out at her and shout wretched insults as she passed by. But Madalyne was too vain to give a damn, she just ignored them and strutted proudly on by. As for Madame Dupree, she pretty much stayed out of Madalyne's way and let her carry out her business in any manner she chose. She was after all her bread and butter. The 25% earnings that Madame Dupree received from the classy call girl kept Bardow Parlors in operation.

Madalyne considered most men to be nothing more than shallow, gluttonous slobs with only three things on their minds: Strong drink, red meat and loose women. To her men were just dull, disgusting, horny little pigs that could be discarded like rubbish. But Madalyne felt much differently about Sir Francis. She thought highly of him and treated the baron with the utmost dignity and respect. He was extraordinarily handsome, sophisticated and distinguished gentleman, always kind and courteous and cherished her dearly.

After nearly a year of courtship Sir Francis Draconian and Madalyne Vandeveer were finally married in Saint James Church. The wedding ceremony was extravagant and glorious with over a hundred of their wealthy aristocratic friends in attendance. The reception banquet later that evening was held in the ballroom at Draconian Palace on Cromwell Road and included some of the finest exotic cuisine in all of Europe. The atmosphere was gay and festive with plenty of song and dance and an overabundance of brandy and vintage wines from France and Italy. Later that evening there was a massive orgy with many well-known celebrities and other distinguished guests from all over England. The wild party lasted all night. Madame Dupree and all her strumpets from Bardow Parlors were there providing non-stop entertainment for all the wealthy barons and magnates.

One evening while traveling abroad conducting business in

the Mediterranean port town of Marseilles in southern France, Sir Francis Draconian was robbed by a couple of thugs near the docks and left for dead. His body was found floating in the bay by some passersby the next morning and his remains were sent back to London for interment in Saint James Abbey. Sir Francis Draconian and Madalyne Vandeveer bore no children, nor did they have any living relatives, which according to his will made Madalyne the sole beneficiary of the baron's estate and the spacious twenty-five room Draconian Palace in Kensington.

To go along with her enchanting charm and radiant beauty was the harlot's strange supernatural ability to vanish at will or mysteriously turn men into stone. She was well practiced in the ancient art of magic and witchcraft and could seduce even the most savage of brute or beast with just one glance from her piercing blue eyes. As a sorceress Madalyne delved deeply into the occult, conjuring up spirits, casting spells on unsuspecting victims, and even reading men's minds. Sometimes she would invoke or unknowingly attract the ghosts of the undead like vampires, werewolves, and other shadowy shape-shifting fiends. Even the foulest of evil spirits and demons from the underworld found it favorable to follow the young temptress around and terrify anybody who came near. On one occasion while shopping for lace scarves and shawls in the fancy boutiques on London's posh west side, Madalyne was ambushed by a pair of mudlarks who were intent on robbing and ravishing her. When they came at her to tear off her clothes, she simply looked them in the eyes and they fainted where they stood and turned to stone.

Weary of leading the life of a wealthy widow, Madalyne Vandeveer secured the services of a broker to liquidate her assets and sell the elaborate Draconian Palace she had inherited and purchase a quaint little cottage by the sea near Dover in Kent. One day Madalyne took no less than a half dozen strongmen to guard and protect her, climbed aboard her elegant calash, and set off through the English countryside toward the coast. Now she was perfectly capable of protecting herself from just about anything. The escorts were nothing more than a display of power and prosperity who went along strictly for her own amusement. Along the way she would entertain herself by putting on peep shows for the rough and tumble guards just to pass the time knowing that she could have any one of them any time she pleased. Madalyne enjoyed watching them get aroused and all worked up as they watched her strip through the carriage window. Their insatiable lust and frustration for her burning up inside them like an unquenchable fire. Outside her ethereal beauty could tame even the wildest of savages, but inside her scandalous heart was like a ravenous wolf, full of contempt. When they finally reached their destination she opened up her coffers and paid the escorts quite handsomely then sent them on their way knowing perfectly well that they would just waste it all away on strong drink and the comfort of the cheap floozies waiting in the alleys.

When Madalyne was out and about in Dover the townspeople would stop and stare as she passed by. The woman and children scoffed at her from the street corners while the young men flocked around and tried to proposition her in any way they could. She rode into Dover one day with much fanfare and everybody in town knew who she was, where she had come from, and all about her lavish lifestyle and promiscuous past. What they didn't know was that Madalyne Vandeveer was a powerful and cunning witch with a wicked heart and a bitter distaste for men.

Sometimes when the weather was fair Madalyne and her entourage would make the day-long journey to Maidstone and lodge for the night in the most luxurious inn with full accommodations. If it was sunny, the next day she would visit Penenden Heath, notorious site of the hangings of a handful of accused witches in the mid 1600's. This always raised a lot of eyebrows from the townspeople, especially the archbishop and magistrates who followed her around from stone to stone.

Oftentimes Madalyne would take the ferry across the channel to France or Belgium and hire a chaperone to chauffeur her into Paris or Brussels, always lodging in the most luxurious suites at the fanciest chateaus. In the evening she would glide vagariously through the streets of the red light district to enjoy the hustle and bustle of the nightlife, attracting attention wherever she went. Sometimes she would stop in for a drink or two at the secret swanky underground nightclubs around town to mingle with her old vampyre friends and other nefarious creatures. On one occasion, while Madalyne was away in Paris, the archbishop and all the magistrates in and around Dover and Maidstone consorted to devise a clever plot that they might falsely accuse her of some callous and dreadful transgression and put her to death. In her absence they dispatched a spy to Folkstone to watch for the ferry returning from Calais. Later that night they disguised themselves in hooded cloaks and masqueraded under the cover of darkness to Penenden Heath to desecrate the graves of the heretics that Madalyne loved. They opened up thirteen of the unholy graves and removed the detached skulls. Then they surreptitiously carried them back to Dover and buried them in a circle in the woods behind Madalyne's cottage to make it appear like some bizarre and twisted ritual that she had performed.

Two days later word came from the lookout that Madalyne's ferry had docked in Folkstone and that she was on her way back to Dover. The spy followed her into town, staying about five furlongs behind so as not to be noticed. When Madalyne arrived back at her cottage later that evening, the archbishop and magistrates were waiting with constables to arrest her. They falsely accused her of witchcraft and necrophilia for digging up and desecrating the graves at Penenden Heath. When she heard the news she wept hysterically and flatly denied knowing anything about it, claiming that she had been out of town so how could she have anything to do with the crimes? The constables detained her nonetheless and brought in the bloodhounds to search her property. It didn't take them long to sniff out the skulls buried in the woods. They immediately arrested Madalyne, whipped her thirteen times and threw her into a dungeon for the night. The following morning they brought her back to the cottage in shackles. But instead of hanging or burning her at the stake as was the customary practice for executing those convicted of witchcraft in these days, they chained her up inside a coffin and clandestinely buried her alive in the middle of the skull circle, leaving her to die in agony. Her tormented moans and desperate cries for help could be heard coming from the woods all night until she finally succumbed the next day.

To this day it is rumored by many that the ghost of Madalyne Vandeveer still haunts these woods. It has been reported that her desperate and agonizing cries for mercy left unanswered can still be heard coming from the woods at night. For nearly two and a half centuries since Madalyne's execution, there have been numerous sightings of strange and eerie specters and ghost-like figures near the site of where her old cottage once stood. The cottage has long since disappeared, but the woods are purported by many to be haunted by evil spirits, including the wayward ghost of Madalyne Vandeveer.

COUNTY LIBRARY

~Premise~

What if I told you there are creatures in this world so cunning and so clever that they can stalk their prey for days, weeks, months, even years without being detected. Would you believe me? These creatures are the ultimate masters of disguise and can hide behind their masks of false identity for as long as they please. Still not convinced? Some of these creatures have been around for hundreds, perhaps thousands of years, tormenting their unsuspecting victims and driving them to the brink of madness.

"Blood is rushing,
Temperature is rising,
Sweating from my brow.
Like a snake her body fascinates me,
I can't look away now."

Stop! Stop! Stop!
The Hollies, 1966

This whole crazy nightmare began with a chance encounter at, of all places, the County Library. In the evenings after work I would often go down to the Central Branch to conduct research and make printouts, or to just relax in the lounge and read a good book. I was told it was also a great place to meet pretty girls. After a long day at the mausoleum, I would strap on my backpack and make the short walk to the library with a pocketful of coins and search for interesting articles and reports to copy.

There was this one exceptionally attractive girl who had caught my eye on several occasions. She visited the library a few times a week and I would always see her sitting all alone at her favorite table with a stack of books by her side. One Thursday evening I spotted her just sitting there reading a textbook and jotting down notes. Now normally I'm quite shy, a loner and not much of a social butterfly, but for some reason or another I remember feeling a bit bolder than usual that night, so I went over and sat down across from her to get a better look. She glanced over at me and smiled as I fumbled through my backpack for something to read. She must have been in her mid-twenties and looked as though she was from the Middle East or of Mediterranean descent. She had long, black hair that was braided and pulled back in a ponytail, and her olive-colored skin was as smooth as Sahara sand. Her almond-shaped eyes were dark and exotic and reminded me of opals or black onyx stones. She wore dark eyeshadow and mascara and her lashes were long and luscious. Dangling around her neck was a shiny gold chain with a beautiful teardrop-shaped emerald pendant which sparkled brilliantly beneath the artificial lighting.

For the next fifteen minutes or so we continued playing our little game of peekaboo, I see you too, but I was too nervous to strike up a conversation. We exchanged a few more friendly glances, then she got up to leave. I watched her out the corner of my eye as she gathered up her things and headed for the lobby. When I looked down, I noticed she had left her library card behind. I reached across the table to snatch it up and read the name on the back. Her name was Maggie. I looked up to see if I could catch her, but she was already out the door. I grabbed my stuff and ran outside. I caught up with her just as she was backing out of the parking lot and rapped lightly on the passenger side window. She turned with a startled look on her face and I held the card up against the glass so she could see it. She leaned over to roll down the window. "Excuse me. I didn't mean to alarm you, but I think you forgot your library card," I said and politely handed her the card.

She rolled her eyes apologetically, and in a thick Middle Eastern accent, said, "Oh silly me! I swear I'd lose my head if it weren't screwed on tight.. Thank you very much!"

"No problem," I said. "It was my pleasure." She rolled up her window, blew me an affectionate kiss, and sped off. When I got back inside I wrote her name and license plate number on a piece of scrap paper and crammed it in my coat pocket.

The following day I rushed home, put on some clean clothes, and hurried down to the library to see if Maggie was around. When I got there at about 7 o'clock, she was already relaxing in the lounge reading her book. I slipped in without her noticing and hid nervously behind the bookshelves. After several tense and indecisive moments, I finally worked up enough courage to walk over to where she was sitting. I pulled out the chair right next to her and calmly sat down. She looked surprised to see me. "Oh it's you....Hi! I was hoping you'd show up. I really wanted to thank you for returning my library card yesterday."

"You already did," I said.

"Well, that was sure kind of you."

"It was no trouble at all, really," I assured her. "You must be Maggie?"

"Yes."

"Hi, Maggie. It's nice to meet you. My name is Tommy, by the way." I extended my hand.

"It's very nice to meet you too, Tommy."

"You sure come here often. Are you a student at the university or something?" I asked, glancing down to see what she was reading.

Underneath her long raincoat she had on a flowered blouse, an oh so tight-fitting miniskirt, some black fishnet stockings, and a pair of laced up leather boots. "Yes, I'm a foreign exchange student from London. I'm here for a year taking some psychology courses."

"Oh how interesting. Anything else?" I asked.

"Well let's see. I play flute at the conservatory on the weekends. How about you, Tommy? Are you a student as well? I don't recall ever seeing you around campus before."

"No, not me. I just come here to do research in my spare time," I explained, careful not to reveal too much.

She shifted in her seat, looked at me curiously, and said, "You know, I've been here almost every night for the past two weeks. I'm really getting sick and tired of this place. What do you say we get out of here and go somewhere where we can get to know each other a little better?"

I was flabbergasted. "Are you suggesting we…"

She cut me off before I could finish. "I'm suggesting that we get out of this tomb and go for a ride or something a little more stimulating. I wanna do something exciting for a change. Anything other than this." She slammed her book shut, stuffed it in her handbag, stood up and said, "Are you coming or not…?"

"Sure, why not," I anxiously agreed. "I'm pretty sick of this place myself." I quickly collected my things and followed her out the door.

Maggie's car was parked in the exact same spot as the previous day, and she was a beauty too. It was a sky blue Mercury Comet convertible. A real classic from the early 60's, and it was in mint condition. She unlocked the doors and said, "Go ahead, Tommy. Hop in."

Feeling slightly apprehensive, I opened the passenger door and sat down. The interior was immaculate like it had just rolled off the assembly line. It smelled faintly of jasmine and vanilla. "Nice ride you have here," I said.

"Oh thanks. I inherited it from my grandmother after she passed away. As you can see she kept it in tip-top shape."

"So where are you taking me anyway?" I asked.

"Oh, I don't know. Where would you like to go?" she said as she fired up the engine. The old V6 roared to life, but idled smoothly and purred like a kitten. "I have a full tank of gas. I thought we could drive around town for a while, maybe park somewhere and watch the moonrise. What do you think?"

"Sounds good to me," I replied. It was just getting dark so we cruised around for a little while until we reached the top of Beacon Hill where we could see the moon coming up over the horizon. She put the car in park, switched off the headlights, and calmly shut down the engine. She unbuckled her seatbelt and reclined back in her seat. I did the same trying not to act nervous. "Beautiful isn't it?" I said. But she didn't respond. "So, do you live in one of those dorms on campus?" I finally asked.

"No, I rent a small flat nearby."

"Have any roommates?" I inquired.

"Nope. I live alone. I prefer it that way. Nice and quiet and no wild parties to contend with."

"I hear that. I'm not much of a party animal either," I admitted.

We sat together just staring at the full moon for a minute or two, then she looked over at me and said, "How about you, Tommy. Do you live by yourself?"

"Yeah. I have a one bedroom apartment just a few blocks from the library," I told her.

Maggie fidgeted, batted her eyelashes, and said playfully, "Would you like to come up to my place and have a drink? It's not very far from here and I don't really have anything to do tonight."

I was stunned. Here I was, sitting alone in the dark with a beautiful girl I just met who was obviously dressed for more than just a night out at the local library, up on Lovers Lane watching the moonrise, and now she's just invited me up to her place for cocktails? I couldn't believe it. Doing my best not to sound overly excited, I said, "Um, sure. I guess so. I don't have any plans." She smiled sweetly, fired up the Mercury, and coasted down the hill back into town. Could this be my lucky day? It had been a long time since a pretty girl had taken me home. A few minutes later she pulled into a driveway down on College Way. She lived on the second floor of a quaint little duplex only a mile or two from the university.

When we got up to her place she told me to make myself comfortable while she went and fetched us something to drink.

I flopped down on the big fluffy sofa and looked around the apartment. Maggie sure had some pretty cool stuff. There was a charming set of crystal candelabras and some hand painted flower vases which looked as though they were from ancient Greece. Hanging on the wall by the doorway was a fancy egg-shaped antique mirror, and on the bookshelf was an expensive Kenwood receiver with big old floor speakers in every corner of the room. And lining the wall behind the brass music stand were a dozen or so framed photographs. Curious, I set my backpack down and walked over to have a closer look. It was a series of black and whites, and they were all of Maggie dressed in a skimpy outfit belly dancing at what appeared to be some kind of shabby cabaret. I should have known. The snapshots were extremely racy and featured Maggie in a sequence of very provocative poses. She looked absolutely ravishing. I wondered if she had Gypsy blood running through her veins. At closer inspection I noticed a pair of real shady looking characters lurking around the stage. They were both wearing trench coats and Fedoras and could have easily passed for a couple of gangsters or underworld spies. I suddenly became very suspicious. Were they Maggie's bodyguards? I felt concerned and a little uneasy and wondered if maybe my little Egyptian goddess was into something other than just belly dancing. Something a little more illicit, more sinister, more...dangerous.

Just then she returned with a couple of drinks. She cleared her throat as she entered the room to get my attention. "Are you through feasting your eyes now?" she said amusingly.

"Sorry," I replied nervously. "I was just admiring your pictures."

"I can see that."

"I didn't realize you were a belly dancer too. Very impressive," I said as I crossed the room and sat back down.

"A girl's gotta make a living." She set the drinks down on the coffee table, "Is whiskey alright?"

"Yes, that's fine. Thank you." I nodded my head and took a sip. "So when were those taken? They look pretty recent," I asked.

"They were taken about a year ago by a dear friend of mine

at a place in Soho called Nephthys Nightclub. Do you like them? There's plenty more where they came from."

I wondered what she meant by that. I considered questioning her about the nefarious-looking spooks in the photos, but thought better of it. "Nice place you have here," I said instead.

"Oh, thanks. I really like it here. It's nice and cozy, don't you think?" she said suggestively. She took off her London Fog and draped it over the back of the sofa and sat down right beside me. Our eyes locked. I remember thinking, this must be how Mark Antony felt when he first laid eyes on Cleopatra. Acting on impulse, I decided to make my move. I inched closer and leaned forward to kiss her, but she put her fingers gently against my lips and said teasingly, "Uh, uh, uh. Not so fast, Tommy. I have something I want to show you first.." Suddenly she stood up, slowly strutted to the other side of the room and switched off the lights. She went over to the stereo and turned on some soft music. Then she took a matchbox from the bookshelf and lit a pair of scented candles.

She reached up to let her hair down, my eyes never leaving her gaze. She gave her pretty head a shake and her long, silky hair fell down loosely across her shoulders. I was spellbound. She slowly rolled her hips and started swaying seductively in time to the music. Little by little the volume grew louder and louder, the rhythm faster and faster until the music reached a fever pitch and Maggie was whirling around wildly in a mad frenzy as if she were possessed.

The music stopped abruptly and a deathly silence suddenly fell over the apartment. She licked her lips and grinned mischievously like she wanted to play. I was left there starstruck and tongue-tied, unable to speak. She started unbuttoning her blouse, pointed, and waved her finger for me to come closer.

That's when things started going horribly wrong and spiraling out of control. I set my half-empty glass down on the coffee table and tried to stand up, but for some reason I felt groggy and lightheaded and thought I was going to pass out. I finally made it to my feet and started staggering toward her. Everything looked fuzzy and I was getting dizzy. I tripped and fell over the table, nearly spilling our drinks, and blacked out. The last thing I remember before I hit the floor was thinking, is this what she wanted to show me or was there something more?

When I came to about an hour later, I was lying face up on Maggie's bed and my coat and shoes were gone. The room was dark and shadowy except for the faint glow of the full moon filtering through the open window and a couple of candles flickering in the breeze. My head was still throbbing from where I must have bumped it on the way down, and I felt sick to my stomach. After a moment or two I was finally able to focus a little better. And that's when I noticed Maggie standing over by the bed just smiling down on me with that mischievous grin of hers. She was wearing a white cotton bathrobe that reached all the way down to her feet, and I couldn't help but to wonder what, if anything, she had on underneath. I tried to sit up, but my legs were numb and I felt paralyzed, as if I were strapped to the bed. "What did you put in my drink, Maggie?" I demanded to know. She didn't say anything. "How long have I been lying here?" She didn't say a word, she just stood there floating silently like a ghostly silhouette in the pale moonlight. I glanced around and noticed that the bedroom door was latched tight. "How did I get in here anyway? I don't remember a thing. Wait…Did you carry me in?"

Her smirk widened, "Yes," was all she said. She reached down to untie the sash from around her waist and the robe fell to the floor. She was completely naked except for the gold necklace. I tried to take her all in, but my eyes were getting heavy and I drifted off. A second later my eyes snapped open, but Maggie was not there anymore. "I'm over here, Tommy," I heard her whisper. I slowly turned my head and there she was again. But this time she was lying on her side with her head propped up in one of those provocative poses just smiling away all innocent like, as if nothing had happened.

Suddenly she got up on all fours and started creeping toward me, licking her lips as if she were some kind of wild animal stalking its prey. I tried to roll off the bed, but I was frozen in place, trapped and defenseless like an ordinary house fly caught in a black widow's deadly web of deceit. I must have dozed off again or blinked for a split second because when I opened my eyes, Maggie was not Maggie anymore, she was a mangled ball of matted dog hair, slimy fish scales, ruffled bird feathers, and twisted tentacles. I tried desperately to escape the unspeakable horror, but I couldn't move a muscle in my body. All I could do was lay there helplessly and watch in utter shock as she underwent a series of hideous transformations; shifting back and forth, morphing in and out of various repulsive and unrecognizable half-human/half-creature mutations. What had once been a beautiful dark-skinned temptress, was now an appalling conglomeration of misshapen eyes, gaping mouths, and slithery tongues.

Out of the darkness a bright flash followed by a soft explosion of refracting light fragments suddenly shattered the silence, showering the room with a million snippets of broken glass. The spontaneous pop snapped me back to my senses. By the Grace of God I somehow managed to muster up enough strength to free myself from her icy grip and rolled off the bed. I landed hard on the floor with a muffled thud and started crawling across the carpet on my hands and knees.

Suddenly a tangled mess of foul smelling tentacle-like appendages shot out from under the bed, making a disgusting sucking sound as they probed the darkness like deformed umbilical cords searching for something to strangle. The door seemed a million miles away. I'd never make it in time. Spreading through the room like slimy tendrils, one of them found me, then another, wrapping themselves tightly around my ankles and pulling me across the carpet. I fought desperately to break free, but they squeezed even harder and slowly dragged me closer to the bed. I felt around frantically for something - anything I could use to ward off this monstrosity and found my shoes. I picked one up and started whacking the tentacles over and over as hard as I could. They twitched and squirmed and finally loosened their grip just long enough for me to scoot backwards on my hands and knees until my back was flat up against the wall. She made a dreadful gurgling noise and suddenly the tentacles came at me again, and this time they were going for my throat. I had all I could take. I stood up, scrambled over to the window, and jumped.

The next day I woke up in the ER at University Park Hospital with the worst hangover I have ever had and some pretty significant injuries, including a broken leg, dislocated shoulder, a fractured collarbone, and a severe concussion. The doctor said I was lucky to be alive. Evidently some passersby spotted me lying unconscious in the grass and called 911. I wonder what those nosy librarians would think if they could see me now? I had been drugged and there were cuts and scrapes all over my body. I had several bruised ribs which made it extremely difficult to breathe. I was suffering from a severe case of rug burn on my backside, and of course, some nasty lacerations on both of my ankles. "And Tommy," the doctor said. "We have decided to place you under suicide watch until we've determined exactly what happened out there. You should never mix barbiturates with alcohol. It can be a very lethal combination."

SALT CREEK

In 1992, the year I was to marry my high school sweetheart, an urgent letter arrived from a former colleague at the Royal Academy of Herpetology informing me about the possible sighting of a new extant species of giant salamander in the ancient redwood forest of northern California. As you might expect, the prospect of such a revolutionary discovery had the scientific community buzzing with excitement. As assistant and former colleague of Professor Filbert's, I had the privilege of collaborating with him on several groundbreaking studies involving the paleogeographic life history of giant salamanders in Asia and North America, and was quite familiar with the evolution and ancestry of these prehistoric tetrapods. So it was no surprise when I received his invitation to join him on an all-expense paid expedition to investigate these claims.

Sylvia and I had been practically inseparable since graduating college in 1985. I was the love of her life, the apple of her eye, so you can well imagine her disappointment and heartbreak when I announced my plans to travel abroad and take part in the expedition. I explained it was the opportunity of a lifetime, the chance to fulfil a lifelong dream, and after nearly a week of sweet talking and intelligent reasoning, she reluctantly gave in to my wishes. On the day of my departure, she even drove me to the airport and sent me off with an affectionate hug and kiss goodbye.

The flight from Heathrow to the west coast of the United States was long and boring, so I slept for a few hours to pass the time until my arrival in San Francisco. The Herpetological Society reserved a suite for me at the Hyatt Hotel with a magnificent view of the bay, and they graciously paid for all of my food, travel, and lodging expenses. The following day I boarded a northbound Amtrak to Eureka and on to our base camp in Weaverville. Our outpost was actually located on a state-run campground just a couple of miles from town under the shadow of majestic Mount Shasta. Upon my arrival I was greeted by a couple of young, ambitious interns as they were loading equipment and supplies into a rented van. Just then Professor Filbert stepped out of the cabin and hurried over to shake my hand. "Manny! So good to see you again, my friend. Thanks for coming all this way at such short notice. How was your flight?"

"Pleasantly smooth and uneventful. How are you, professor?"

"Tired. Excited but tired. These past few days of last minute preparations have worn me out I'm afraid. Nothing a good night's sleep won't cure. You must be hungry, Manny. What do you say we go into town and grab a bite to eat…? I'll fill you in on the details along the way."

Originally established in 1850 as a gold mining settlement, Weaverville was now a recreational hotspot for outdoor enthusiasts and a popular destination for campers, hunters and fishermen. "Congratulations on your new post as Director and Curator of Herpetology at the Metro Zoo, by the way."

"Thanks! Luckily I have been blessed with a loyal assistant I can depend on to run the show while I am away."

"I also understand that you and Sylvia are engaged to be married?"

"Yes, we are. We plan on tying the knot this summer. I do hope you'll attend the wedding, professor?" I said. "We will send you an official invitation, of course."

"Of course! I wouldn't miss it for the world."

"So professor, what's the plan out here? I want the full rundown."

"Well Manny, I'll give it to you simply. Our primary objective is to investigate and ultimately verify a pair of recent sightings of what's been described as an unusually large salamander wandering around down by the Eel River. Our goal is to collect data and catalogue any type of evidence we happen to find that could potentially help support these claims, such as tracks, bones, teeth or anything tangible which can be documented and brought back to the lab for analysis. Ideally, the best case scenario would be to capture this creature alive, if it really exists, or at least photograph it in its natural habitat, and find out if there are more.

"Have you spoken to any of the eyewitnesses?" I asked.

"Not personally. They were interviewed by a couple of park rangers and a wildlife biologist the day of the alleged sightings. I have copies of their statements. They claim the animal they saw was between ten and fifteen feet long and walked like a giant Dicamptodon."

"That's impossible!" I objected. "That's the size of a full grown crocodile, for Christ's sake. The largest Dicamptodon on record is only fifteen inches long, and the Asian giants only reach five feet max."

"I know, I know. It all sounds a little crazy, but remember those reports in the old Cryptozoological journals about a giant salamander wandering around in the Trinity Alps? Maybe those stories are true after all."

Later that evening, when we returned to camp, Professor Filbert handed me a stack of papers, including the eyewitnesses' accounts and a couple of USGS maps of the area where the alleged sightings had occurred. "These are for your reading pleasure. I highly suggest we retire early tonight so that we are well rested. We'll be rolling out of here tomorrow at sun up."

The next morning we climbed into the van and drove about sixty miles in a southwesterly direction along Route 162 through the ancient limestone formations until we were deep in the coastal redwood forest of Mendocino County. The plan was to take a series of three day hikes to the designated sites with one or two days of rest in between. Bears and cougars were common in these parts, so we decided it would be safer to all stick together rather than splitting up. Our first excursion was to the location where the most recent sighting had occurred. A medium-sized tributary of the Eel River called Salt Creek, approximately twelve hundred feet above sea level near the small town of Covelo.

Professor Filbert was an average sized fellow in his mid-forties. He had traveled all over the world and although he was a good six or seven years my senior, he was in terrific shape, no doubt due in part to his twenty plus years in the field surveying frogs and salamanders. Before we set out to Salt Creek, he gathered us together in a circle and said, "The Forest Service has been kind enough to provide each of us with a two-way radio and a secure frequency to the nearest ranger station in the event of an emergency. GPS trackers have also been provided in case we happen to get lost or stranded, as well as a couple of very loud pop guns to ward off any potential predators."

The torrential rain and misty fog that hung perpetually over the ancient forest was relentless, and the damp, rugged terrain made traversing up and down steep, slippery slopes treacherous at best.

The first day we managed to capture and release a total of five Dicamptodon salamanders in the matter of six hours' time, including two rather large adult morphs measuring between six and eight inches. The other four specimens were medium-sized larval forms that we discovered while overturning stones in the creek.

The second day we drove into Covelo and ate a hearty breakfast before venturing back out to Salt Creek. Over breakfast we decided it might be wise to split up into pairs after all so we could cover more ground. We agreed to stay within a hundred yards of each other at all times and to check in every thirty minutes. Our objective was to search a five mile radius around Salt Creek where the first alleged sighting had taken place just over a month ago. Professor Filbert took one of his technicians, a pretty, young intern named Carolyn and hiked downstream to check the creek, while Peter and I started rolling logs. The heavy rains tapered off but the thick fog persisted, making visibility difficult and at times downright dangerous. Peter and I didn't see any morphs that day, but Professor Filbert and Carolyn did capture a nine inch paedomorph swimming around at the bottom of Salt Creek.

The third day we decided to switch partners, which meant I had the distinct pleasure of teaming up with Carolyn, the lovely, young wildlife biologist, which I didn't mind a bit. I believe I may have even blushed when she smiled and told me how much she admired my work. The day started off crisp and a little on the cool side, but by mid-morning the sun had burned off most of the marine layer and the moisture from the previous night's rain still clung to the lush, green undergrowth.

After a quick lunch break and a short rest, we again split up to search for clues. All of a sudden Professor Filbert's exhilarated voice crackled over the radio. "Manny…Carolyn…Come quick! We found something down here. You're not going to believe this. Hurry, please!" We gathered up our gear and ran as fast as we could to see what all the fuss was about. Professor Filbert met us halfway down the hillside, and he was ecstatic. "We found a set of tracks in the mud!" When we got down to the creek Peter was circling clockwise around a small section of the stream bank taking shots from various angles with his Polaroid.

"Sweet Mother of God!" I shouted. "Look at the size of those things. They're enormous!" The impressions looked as though they had been made by some kind of prehistoric metoposaurus, but I knew right away they were the footprints of a very large Dicamptodon, and by the looks of them, they couldn't have been more than a few hours old.

"Carolyn, would you take some measurements, please? We need the length and width of both the front and hind feet, as well as each individual digit. Please be very careful. We don't want to ruin a single print." Professor Filbert could hardly contain himself. "Well Manny, what do you think about our extraordinary discovery? I'm certainly no expert when it comes to tracks and bones, but those are unmistakingly the footprints of an extremely large Dicamptodon salamander, of that I am quite sure."

"Yes professor, you are absolutely right. And look, they lead straight into the creek. What do you propose we do now?" I asked.

Shielding his eyes against the bright sunshine, he looked up to the sky and said, "Our first priority must be to preserve and protect these tracks as best we can. If it rains it could wash them away for good. Do you have anything we can use to cover them up with?"

I reached down, unzipped my backpack and pulled out a plastic rain tarp. "This should do the trick," I said as I unfolded it and spread it out on the ground.

"Perfect! If we stake it down it should cover the majority of the prints and keep them dry until we can render some casts. Are you kids almost finished down there?"

"Yes sir. I took twelve shots from four different angles and they all came out clear. Here, take a look," Peter said excitedly and handed them to him.

"Carolyn, my dear...Did you get some accurate measurements for us?"

"Yes professor, I did. The tracks appear to have all the earmarks consistent with that of an extremely large urodele. The quadrupeds look to be around fifteen and a quarter inches and the hind feet sixteen and a half inches. The longest digit on the back foot is approximately nine and a half inches. Still working on the width, sir."

"Holy shit!" I said. That means we are talking about a tetrapod somewhere between ten and fifteen feet, just as the eyewitnesses described. I'll bet it must weigh seven or eight hundred pounds, maybe more. An animal of that proportion would be capable of swallowing a small doe!"

"Professor Filbert...?"

"Yes, Carolyn?"

"There are also what appear to be tail drag marks. Shall I measure them as well?"

"Absolutely! Thank you." Professor Filbert paused for a minute, scratched his chin and said, "Alright...Listen up everybody. There's been a slight change of plans in light of our recent discovery. Rather than taking the day off tomorrow, we need to come back out and make some casts. We will be taking Friday and Saturday off instead. Any objections...? Good! Now let's get those tracks covered up before it starts to rain. Carolyn, did you get some measurements on those drag marks?"

"Yes, professor. The swath of the drag marks indicate a tail length of just under six and a half feet."

"Nicely done. Let's get them covered up so we can head back into town for an early dinner. I don't know about you, but I'm famished!"

Over dinner the four of us sat down to discuss our options. We considered setting some kind of trap, but decided it would just be too risky. We even contemplated coming out at night to snap some pictures of the beast, but without the right equipment at our disposal, there just didn't seem any use. In the end we all agreed it would probably be best to deploy primitive hunting techniques and simply stake out the area to see if we could catch a glimpse of this elusive creature. When we returned to camp later that evening Professor Filbert gave us a firm warning. "And remember, folks. Not a word to anyone about what we are doing out here until this investigation is complete. Is that understood? If word gets out that there is some kind of prehistoric amphibian running around in these woods, this place would be overrun with news reporters and local thrill-seekers in no time."

At the crack of dawn we hiked the all too familiar Trillium Trail back to Salt Creek and made it there in less than an hour. And on this trip we took with us a ten pound bag of quick-set casting mix, a couple of buckets, and some trowels Professor Filbert had purchased at the local hardware store.

First we pulled up the stakes and uncovered the tracks to make sure they were still in the same good condition as we had left them the day before. Dipping cold water from the creek, we worked in pairs mixing and pouring the four plaster casts, one for each foot. When we finished, about an hour later, we covered them back up and sat down for a snack while we waited for them to harden. The plan was to stash the ten pound casts in plastic bags and retrieve them on Sunday when we didn't have all the extra equipment to weigh us down.

Without warning an odd whooshing sound came up from the

bottom of the creek and Carolyn shrieked at the top of her lungs. There was a loud splash and the giant salamander we had spent the last three days searching for suddenly lunged from the water and snapped its enormous jaws, nearly snagging Carolyn by her leg. Instinctively I wrapped myself tightly around her waist and pulled her out of the way just in the nick of time, and we both tumbled to the ground. The fifteen foot creature made a peculiar gulping noise as it drew in oxygen and started swinging its enormous tail from side to side. It suddenly snapped its massive head forward and sprung at Peter, who was standing by the creek with his mouth wide open looking on with utter amazement. He screamed and scampered up the slick embankment, narrowly escaping the prehistoric amphibian's powerful jaws and rows of bone-crushing teeth. Without further ado, Professor Filbert pulled out his pop gun and fired off three shots in rapid succession. The giant salamander flinched and stopped dead in its tracks and we saw this as our opportunity to climb up the embankment to safety. The beast assumed an aggressive defensive posture then slowly retreated into the water, swaying its gargantuan tail back and forth like a paddle before disappearing beneath the swift current. We were all in a state of shock and couldn't decide whether the beast was just hungry or merely trying to defend its territory.

"Phew, that was close! Is everybody OK? Carolyn, are you hurt?"

"No professor, I'm fine. Just a little shaken is all."

"How about you, Peter?"

"No sir. But I'm afraid the tracks are ruined."

"Well, I guess seeing really is believing after all, huh professor? Looks like Father Hubbard and all the other eyewitnesses were telling the truth all along. What do you suggest we do now?" I asked.

"I recommend we terminate this investigation immediately and vacate Salt Creek quickly as possible before one of us becomes lunch for that...that behemoth! Once things have settled down, I'll dispatch somebody to retrieve the casts. For now we must keep a tight lid on this and not speak a word of it to anybody. Am I clear?"

We all shook our heads in agreement.

When I arrived at Heathrow three weeks ahead of schedule, my fiancée was anxiously waiting to pick me up. "Well, honey…Did you find your giant salamander?" she said sarcastically.

I put my around her, pulled her in close, and said, "I'll tell you all about it on the way home. Now let's get out of here. I'm starving!"

MAGGONA BEACH

In May of 1970, while everybody was singing and dancing to Octopus's Garden, I waltzed into the Museum of Natural History and was immediately escorted to a waiting room on the second floor. The nameplate on the office door to my left read: Dr. Fredrick Stephens, Marine Biologist & Director of Ichthyology, and I knew I was in the right place. I had been summoned by Dr. Stephens just days earlier regarding the possible discovery of a new species of Periophthalmus in the mangrove swamps of southern India.

A few moments later the door swung open and out stepped a distinguished, rather portly gentleman in his mid-fifties with a full beard and mustache, wearing horn-rimmed spectacles and a white lab coat. I stood up to introduce myself and graciously extended my hand. "You must be Doctor Stephens?" I said politely.

"Yes. And you must be Peter. Thanks for dropping by, I've been expecting you. Won't you come in please?" His office was surprisingly small and cramped, his desk cluttered with stacks of textbooks and scientific journals. "Pardon the mess," he said apologetically as he cleared a spot for me to sit. "Things have been rather chaotic around here lately. Please, won't you sit down?"

"Thank you very much."

"Professor Khandir tells me you are quite the adventurer…?" He squinted and scrutinized me for a moment before continuing. "I'm afraid I am a little pressed for time, so let's get right down to business, shall we? A couple of weeks ago I received word that a former associate and dear friend of mine accidentally fell overboard and drowned while on a scuba diving expedition in the

Indian Ocean."

"Oh goodness gracious! How unfortunate. My sincere condolences, sir."

"Yes. Thank you, Peter. He will be sorely missed I assure you. The captain of the diving team claims that Calvin had been acting rather peculiar and even seemed a bit delusional in the hours leading up to his death." Dr Stephens rolled his chair over to an old metal file cabinet, produced a set of keys from his coat pocket, and unlocked one of the drawers. He pulled out a manila envelope and handed it to me, "Evidently the night before his tragic accident he also drew these sketches. Take a look at them and tell me what you think. I'm sure you will find them quite interesting. The good captain said Calvin was raving like a lunatic over dinner about some strange sea creatures he had encountered on one of his earlier dives. Supposedly there were calm seas for the entire duration of the voyage. I fear that he may have deliberately taken his own life."

I opened the envelope and started thumbing through the drawings. I could not believe what I was seeing. "What in pink carnations are these things?" I said emphatically. "Are these for real?" The sketches depicted odd and dreadfully disturbing sea creatures the likes of which I have never seen before and what can only be described as cyclopean cephalopods with big bulging eyes, long tentacles, scaly tail-like appendages, and razor-sharp fangs protruding from the top of their mouths. Several of the sketches depicted dozens of these fishy creatures knotted together in a massive heap of eyeballs, teeth and tentacles.

"I'm sorry, doctor, but I'm a little confused. When we spoke on the phone the other day you said you wanted to talk to me about a new species of Periophthalmus. You didn't mention anything about these drawings."

"My apologies, Peter. I didn't mean to mislead you in any way. It's just that we're trying to keep this sensitive matter under wraps until it can be investigated further. I hope you understand?"

"Of course. But why did you contact me in the first place?"

"Well, Peter, you were highly recommended by Professor

Khandir. She is quite fond of you, you know, and thought that you might like to join her in Ceylon to look into this matter. You know, poke around a bit, see what you can come up with. The museum is prepared to pay you quite handsomely. We would, of course, provide you with all the necessary paperwork, and your travel expenses would be compensated in full should you accept our offer. Accommodations have already been made." He reached into his shirt pocket and handed me a round trip airline ticket, "Your flight is scheduled for the 26th of May, which gives you five days to get ready. Professor Khandir has made arrangements to have you picked up at the airport the following day."

"And will you be coming along too, doctor?" I inquired.

"No, I'm afraid not. This is our busiest time of the year and I have prior commitments here at the museum. We have notified the Ceylonese government about our investigation, so you can expect full cooperation from the local authorities. Oh, and Peter, as I'm sure you are aware, it is monsoon season down there, so be sure to pack extra rain gear and plenty of insect repellent. I hear the mosquitoes can get rather nasty. I think that about covers it. Do you have any questions before I let you go?"

"Yes. How long am I expected to be away?"

"Two, maybe three weeks tops. Anything else?"

"Not that I can think of."

"Good! I will arrange for a taxi to pick you up and take you to the airport. And I will get in touch with Professor Khandir tomorrow to let her know you'll be coming. She'll be absolutely delighted, I'm sure. One more thing, Peter. As an added incentive, the museum is also prepared to reward you with a substantial bonus, a finder's fee if you will, should you happen to capture one or two specimens and bring them back alive in a discreet manner."

The transatlantic plane ride from JFK to Ceylon was long and exhausting, but relatively smooth except for some minor turbulence as we passed over the north African coastline. I had an hour layover in Bombay where the monsoon rains were coming down so hard it felt like a typhoon. The 747 jumbo jet had a bumpy take off, but landed safely in Colombo right on schedule. The cab was already waiting for me outside the terminal.

I arrived at the University of Colombo at 3:30 PM, exactly twelve hours after leaving New York. The Department of Zoology was a large, modern-style facility in the heart of campus. I checked in with the receptionist first and she said Professor Khandir was expecting me. I took the elevator down to the basement and found her in the Marine Sciences Lab tending to her mudskippers just as I knew she would be. She didn't notice me come in so I stood at the doorway and watched her for a minute or two. I first met Professor Agneya Khandir, or 'Aggie' as everybody called her, in Gambia a couple of years earlier and was immediately taken by her good looks. She was a Ceylonese beauty in her mid-thirties with jet black hair, deep wine dark eyes, and a gorgeous hourglass figure. She could have easily been an exotic Indonesian princess, but she was an island girl through and through and I admired her greatly. I set my bags down, "Ahem."

She got all excited when she saw me and came running over to give me an affectionate hug. I squeezed her tight. Ah! The sweet fragrance of cinnamon and citrus fruit was intoxicating. "Peter! There you are, darling. I'm so glad you made it. It's good to see you again."

"It's wonderful to see you again too, Aggie! You're looking fabulous as always."

"Aw, shucks. You're so sweet." She gave me a once over, "You're not looking so bad yourself. Thanks for coming all this way."

"My pleasure! I'm really looking forward to our little adventure in this tropical paradise of yours."

"Come over here! I want to introduce you to our latest newlyweds." I followed her over to a five hundred gallon paludarium filled with mudskippers, or 'blennies' as she liked to call them. "Aren't they adorable? I even named one after you, Peter."

"I'm flattered. You really shouldn't have."

"He reminds me of you. Always chasing the female around," she chortled.

"Real funny, professor," I remarked jokingly.

"Well, I'm sure we'll see a lot more tomorrow."

"I'm sure we will. So where exactly are we going anyway?"

"To a place just down the coast called Maggona Beach. It's only about an hour's drive from here. We'll be lodging at a cozy little bungalow called the Paladin Inn."

"Ooh! Sounds romantic."

She smiled and said, "Now who's being funny? Tomorrow morning we'll go down to the mudflats and have a look around to see if we can find anything unusual. I presume Dr. Stephens showed you the drawings?"

"As a matter of fact, he did. I'm still trying to wrap my head around it. He seems convinced that those creatures of his really are out there. They don't resemble anything I've ever seen before, that's for sure. What do you make of them, Aggie?"

"To tell you the truth, I'm a little skeptical about the whole idea myself. I just hope he's not sending us off on some kind of wild goose chase."

"Me either," I agreed.

"So, yeah, it looks like it's just gonna be the two of us for a couple of days until conditions improve. The captain said the seas are just too choppy to take the vessel out. The dive team is on standby and will be ready to go once this foul weather subsides. As you can well imagine, they are still very distraught over Calvin's tragic death. He was a well-respected and highly-esteemed member of the dive team."

"What the hell happened out there anyway," I asked.

"No one really knows for sure. We're still waiting for the results of the autopsy and toxicology report to come out. They say he got drunk and fell overboard in the middle of the night. They discovered him missing when he didn't show up for breakfast the following morning. The Coast Guard found his body washed up on the beach several days later."

"Dr. Stephens seems to think he may have committed suicide…?"

"I don't think so, Peter. I mean, I didn't really know Calvin very well, but he seemed like a rational person. He was a family man, you know? He was an excellent scuba diver and he had big dreams of piloting his own ship one day and retiring in the Greek Isles."

"Hmm...Did he have a history of sleepwalking or insomnia?"

"Not that I'm aware of, but I guess that's certainly a possibility." She paused for a moment. "Are you ready to go? I just need to stop at my place and pick up my things before we head down there. Here, let me help you with your bags, sir!"

When I first embarked on my journey half a world away on that beautiful spring day in May, I never imagined in my wildest dreams that I would actually encounter these cyclopean cephalopod creatures, let alone do battle with them. Looking back on it now, I realize there is no rational explanation for the bizarre and otherworldly sequence of events I endured that day. As to whether they were merely the figments of an overactive imagination, the drug-induced hallucinations of a heightened state of consciousness, or the hellish visions of a horribly vivid nightmare in which my mind had been altered, I cannot say.

We drove down the coastal highway through the pouring rain in her old beat up Land Rover and got into Maggona Beach before nightfall. We were welcomed graciously by the innkeepers and served a tasty seafood gumbo with tangy curry sauce and hot bread. After dinner the jet lag finally caught up with me and I had to excuse myself early. I conked out as soon as I hit the bed and slept like a log until morning.

Professor Khandir pulled over and parked the Land Rover on the side of the road and started unloading our gear. There was a warm tropical breeze coming off the ocean, but the heavy rain was relentless, the sweltering heat unbearable, and the oppressive humidity stifling, making things just plain miserable. "The estuary is just down on the other side of those mangroves. Once the tides recede we'll be able to slosh around in the mud for as long as we want."

"I take it this isn't your first visit to Maggona Beach?"

"Are you kidding? I was born and raised on this part of the island." She smiled reminiscently and gazed out over the stormy sea. "You know, Peter, when I was younger I was marveled by the wild tales I used to hear about a colossal sea creature roaming around out there in the depths. Turns out it was just an elaborate hoax concocted by the local fishermen to scare off the competition and keep them from dipping their nets in these waters."

We managed to fit all of our equipment into two backpacks, along with some rope in case one of us happened to get stuck in the mud. She pulled out a pair of four foot long bamboo sticks from the back of the Land Rover and handed me one. "These will help us poke our way through the muck and keep us from sinking in too far." Covered from head to toe in rain gear, we slowly made our way down the makeshift trail to Maggona Beach.

Nestled between the bay to the south and a tiny fishing village, whose name I can't even pronounce, to the north, Maggona Beach is nothing more than a narrow strip of shoreline roughly ten miles long and fifty to sixty yards wide where the mouth of the Maggona River empties into the Indian Ocean. On a clear day they say you can see the Maldives from the surrounding hills. But not today.

Even though high tide was not due for another four or five hours, the gale force winds were still powerful enough to produce some pretty hefty waves, kicking up sand in our faces. The patches of mangroves were interspersed with palm trees and some type of tall tropical swamp grass which caused me to sneeze and wheeze, and made wading through the muck extremely challenging. We trudged tirelessly along the beach for a mile or two before finally reaching a network of estuaries and salt marshes. The beach was deserted except for a few blue-footed booby birds. I guess we were the only fools crazy enough to be out in these deplorable conditions. The swamps and mudflats were swollen with rainwater and there were several good sized tide pools that had formed, which looked as though they'd be perfect habitat to search for Periophthalmus. The beach was teeming with all sorts of strange crustaceans, so it was no surprise when we came across a small colony of mudskippers burrowing in and out of the sand. I pulled out my trusty Minolta and started shooting close-ups of the silly little critters as they splashed about from puddle to puddle, foraging for crabs and other arthropods. "Well, there's certainly no shortage of blennies around here, eh professor…?" But she didn't respond. She seemed distracted and looked over my shoulder. Something else had caught her attention.

I turned to see what it was that had Aggie sidetracked. It was a small flock of seagulls and some pelicans circling overhead, and they were swooping down at something very large half-buried in the sand. "What on earth is that…?" I grabbed my binoculars and focused in on the dark object through the mist. At first I thought it might have been a submarine or a downed aircraft. Then I realized what I was seeing. "Holy cow! I think it's a whale carcass. Here take a look."

I passed her the field glasses and she adjusted her sights. "My God! I think you're right. It is a whale, and an awful big one by the looks of it. We better go take a look. Maybe it's still breathing."

We tromped through the mud, the driving rain pelting our hoods, the howling winds buffeting our faces, slowing our pace down to a mere crawl. When we got to within five hundred feet of the carcass, the unmistakable stench of death hit us like a freight train and we had to cover our noses with handkerchiefs. "Good God, that smells horrible." The stench was rancid and we were forced to breathe through our mouths as we crept closer to the rotting mammoth. The foul stench was nauseating and I started to gag. The flies were everywhere and we had to shoo them away just to keep them from going down our throats.

The carcass lay on its side partially submerged in the surf, its stomach and intestines ripped open and disemboweled. We carefully circled around to the front for a closer look. It was the remains of a fifty foot sperm whale, its eyes gouged out of their sockets, its face completely eaten away. Bones had been splintered and the front of its skull had been picked clean. We both took a step back and covered our mouths, but Professor Khandir couldn't hold it in any longer and vomited all over her waders.

Then we saw them, hundreds of them, gnawing at the carcass and scavenging on the chunks of raw flesh they had torn off. They were more terrifying than I ever could have imagined. In fact, they were by far the most repulsive, sickening things I have ever seen and will no doubt haunt my dreams for the rest of my days. They were a dark greenish color with pink and orange pigmentation on their cantaloupe-shaped heads, and they smelled as vile and as wretched as the carcass itself.

There had to be a hundred or more of these cyclopean cephalopod creatures tangled together like spaghetti in one enormous aggregated mass of rolling eyeballs, twisted tentacles and sharp bloody fangs. Their arm-like tentacles were lined with tiny suction cups which they used to cling to the carcass and viciously devour the rotting flesh. The sands of Maggona Beach had been turned into one gigantic grotesque pool of blood, sea foam, slime, whale guts and blubber.

Suddenly a small cluster of these fishy invertebrates started creeping toward us, making a squishy, squashy sound as they skittered across the wet sand. We took another step back, their big protruding eyes watching our every move. And using their flexible tentacles like springboards to propel themselves a good ten or twelve feet in the air, they catapulted. We swatted them away with our bamboo sticks and most of the creatures scattered. But one of them landed at my feet, and in a fit of rage I stomped on it, flattening it like a pancake and proceeded to beat it to death with my flask. It flinched and made a horrible squealing noise as it flopped around in the muck before finally giving up the ghost.

More of them came at us from behind. One of the larger creatures lunged aggressively and latched onto the back of Professor Khandir's leg. She let out a blood-curdling scream as it tore through her clothes and punctured her skin. It dug hard into her flesh, penetrating deeper while she fought desperately to brush it off. "Good God, Peter... Get this damn thing off me!" It wrapped one of its sticky tentacles around her waist and tried dragging her into the surf. She struggled to keep her balance and almost fell into the muck. I rushed over and jabbed the creature repeatedly with the tip of my bamboo stick until I was finally able to pry it loose. The creature fell to the sand, flailed around in the mud for a moment then scuttled off and burrowed itself beneath the carcass.

I snatched Aggie's hand and pulled her out of striking distance. She was having a hard time staying on her feet and I had to half carry her out of harm's way. I ran with her as fast as I could up the slope and found a footpath leading to the highway. Now I say ran, however, if you've ever tried running through mud and sand wearing heavy waders while trying to support an extra hundred and twenty pounds, you know it's more like a slow crawl. Nevertheless, I managed to get us both up the hill to safety, but had to leave poor Professor Khandir waiting by the side of the road while I went and retrieved the Land Rover. She was in excruciating pain and had already lost a lot of blood. I lifted her up and gently placed her in the passenger seat. She was going into shock and I was afraid she might black out. I screeched out of there as fast as I could go and sped off to get help.

Despite a fairly nasty bite mark on her femur and a slight infection, the doctor had Aggie all stitched up and out of the hospital in less than twenty-four hours. The following day we stood in the pouring rain alongside a small group of local villagers on the ridge by the old lighthouse overlooking Maggona Beach and watched as a crew of hazmat workers in protective suits and gas masks bulldozed what was left of the whale carcass back out to sea.

UNCLE SALTY

Lost and adrift on the stormy sea, I awoke from a fitful night's sleep, the remnants of a most dreadful dream still lingering in my clouded subconscious, whereupon I stumbled from my cabin and staggered to the bow of the ship. Unfazed by the wind and waves lashing my face, stinging my eyes with a salty spray, I gripped the rails and gazed out over the water as if in some kind of psychotic daze.

We were miles from port when the squall hit, its gale force winds rocking the Uncle Salty from side to side, flooding the engine room and knocking out power. My fellow crew members had abandoned ship, taking the only lifeboat there was to try and row back to shore. I begged them not to go, but in the end I bid them farewell and watched them fade away into the fog never to be seen or heard from again.

I had been adrift for three days and three nights without a drop of water, subsisting solely on raw tuna and dried cranberries. In desperation I scanned the horizon for any sign of dry land where I might guide the Uncle Salty to safety. Surely somebody must have heard our distress calls and alerted the authorities by now. Through the blanket of fog which spread across the sea like dragon's breath, I could barely make out the contour of forested hills in the distance, and painstakingly steered the vessel in the direction of the rocky shoreline. By now the sails were slashed and torn, flapping wildly in the headwinds, yet somehow the Uncle Salty managed to stay afloat as it tossed and turned across the jetty. But as I neared the beach, the ship scraped up against some jagged rocks and tore open the hull. The galley started taking in water fast, forcing me to jump overboard and swim ashore. When I finally reached the island, I was so tired from treading water that I simply fell to my knees and passed out from exhaustion.

I came to a short time later, shivering and severely dehydrated, with the tides washing over me and realized that if I did not find fresh water soon I may not live to see another day. I dug for clams with my bare hands and traced an SOS in the sand in the hopes a passing plane would spot the shipwreck and radio for help. I found a sturdy piece of driftwood which I fashioned into a spearhead I could use to skewer fish, or as a weapon in the event I happened to cross paths with a tribe of savage cannibalistic headhunters or some wild beast bent on tearing me to shreds, and made my way into the hills in search of fresh water.

It didn't take long before I discovered a bubbling brook where I could cup my hands together and drink freely. Just upstream something stirred in the underbrush. I squinted into the bright sunshine and saw something dark and shadowy creeping along the hillside, something otherworldly, neither beast nor brute, but a creature altogether far more sinister. I could sense it watching me from behind the pines, stalking me, waiting to see what I would do next. I fought the urge to flee at first. But I didn't have a choice, I had to run. And run I did, as fast as my tired feet could carry me all the way back to the beach. I hunkered down behind the biggest boulder I could find to catch my breath and filled my pockets with stones. All that was left of the Uncle Salty was the top of the mast sticking up out of the waves like a flagpole. I was suddenly overcome with a primal fear, a deep-seated fear of living out the rest of my days in isolation on this God-forsaken island, if I survived. A grim sense of hopelessness and despair of living and dying in total obscurity miles from civilization.

Something shiny and metallic caught my eye, glistening in the sun, something quite large and saucer-shaped half-buried in the sand just a few yards away. It made a peculiar humming noise which sounded like a beacon transmitting some kind of low-frequency radio signal. Whatever it was, the object was clearly out of place, unnatural, and not of this world.

From deep in the forest came an awful screeching sound that made my skin crawl. It was unlike anything I had ever heard before, and it was getting closer. I took a handful of stones from my pocket, readied my spear, and stepped out into the open. Hunched down about a hundred yards away was a shaggy, loathsome looking creature of unearthly proportions staring back at me with malevolence. It slowly began creeping toward me on all fours like some kind of prehistoric sloth, twisting and writhing as if it were stricken by epilepsy. The creature was covered in dark brown fur from its head down to its partially webbed feet, with long ape-like limbs which hung all the way to the ground, pronged tusks like those of a warthog, and an elongated elephantine trunk that curled up and down and dragged across the sand.

I knew I'd never be able to outrun this monstrosity, so I stood my ground, armed with my meager arsenal of primitive weapons ready to fight to the death with what was left of my dwindling strength. I began pelting it with stones. The creature twitched and contorted, howling in excruciating pain, but kept slithering closer and closer. It stood up on its hind legs until we were eye to eye and I could smell its foul breath, and started slashing at me, slicing its talon-like claws just inches from my face. Instinctively I backpedaled until I was almost up to my knees in the tide. I sidestepped as the abomination lunged for my throat, lowered my spear and thrust it with all my might deep into the soft tissue of its underbelly, impaling the creature in the wet sand. Then I ran, and ran, and didn't stop running until I reached the other side of the island where I collapsed and passed out on the beach from sheer exhaustion.

And woke up an hour later to the sound of whirling propellers. It was the Coast Guard, at last they had found me.

APPARATUS HILL

When I was a young boy growing up in Jupiter, Florida, every spring break we used to pack up the station wagon and make the long drive up to my Uncle Bud's farm in rural western Pennsylvania. On the edge of his ten acre property was a place called Apparatus Hill where I used to spend a good deal of time bullfrogging in the old fishing hole. In the mid-70's, Apparatus Hill was the site of several reported cattle mutilations at some of the neighboring farms. My family never spoke of the mutilations when I was around, but I had heard. Uncle Bud didn't have any livestock on his farm, just a few chickens. I remember collecting little gray toads in the grassy field and keeping them in jars until he finished mowing, sparing them from certain death.

Over the years I had also heard talk about a character who the locals referred to as the 'Old Hagfish Lady,' a hideous half-woman, half-fish creature that supposedly lived in the pond up on Apparatus Hill. Some even believed she was responsible for the gruesome mutilations and that she kept the severed cow heads as souvenirs. Sometimes as I lay awake at night I would hear strange wailing sounds coming from the woods in back of the cornfields. When I asked my uncle about the noises he would just tell me they were probably owls or coyotes howling at the moon, but I knew better.

The year before my father passed away, which in fact was the last time I would ever see my Uncle Bud, I was out with my fishnet and bucket chasing bullfrogs late one afternoon when I heard something large splashing around in the water at the deep end of the pond. It sounded much too loud to be a bullfrog, and at first I thought it might be a beaver. I crouched down behind a tree stump, stayed perfectly still, and listened for a minute. I looked around to see if I could spot anything moving in the shadows. What I saw made me shudder. It was the figure of a woman bathing in the murky water. She had long scraggly hair, and on each side of her head, where there should have been ears, were long feathery gills. She must have sensed I was watching because she turned her head and slowly stood up. She was completely naked and had slimy green fish scales all over her body. She had to have been ten or twelve feet tall because the water only came up to just above her knees! Suddenly a bullfrog plunged into the pond with a loud splash and she jerked her head around. I saw that as my chance to get out of there and ran as fast I could back to the farmhouse and hid in the basement until dinner time.

    I had a hard time getting to sleep that night. The howling from the woods seemed more terrifying than ever. The next day my curiosity got the best of me, however, and after lunch I ventured back up to Apparatus Hill. The pond looked serene during the day and the trees were full of singing birds. I found a sturdy branch sticking up in the muck, broke it off, and tiptoed over to the deep end of the pond with apprehension. There were lots of large rocks scattered about so I climbed up on the biggest boulder I could find and started probing the stagnant water, gently swirling the algae around. I waited until the water was completely still again, then lowered my head and peered in. Suddenly long wrinkly fingers reached up and grabbed my leg, pulling me under. I struggled to hold my breath as I fought frantically to keep my head above water. She loosened her grip and I clambered out of the pond scared, shivering, and covered with slime, but lucky to escape with my life. I ran back to the farmhouse and hid under the covers for the rest of the day. I never told a soul about my terrifying encounter with the 'Old Hagfish Lady' that day. Nobody ever would have believed me anyway. The next morning my mother asked me why my clothes were soaking wet. I fibbed and told her I slipped and fell into the pond while chasing a bullfrog. I never returned to Apparatus Hill again until.....

Ten years later, I was dating this girl from college by the name of Valerie. She was a local history buff from the Pittsburgh area and when I asked her if she had ever heard of Apparatus Hill or the cattle mutilations, she knew exactly what I was referring to and gave me the strangest look. "Yeah, well guess what? There's been even more mutilations up there recently. I just read about it the other day in the *Gazette*."

"You're kidding, right? My uncle used to have a farm up there. We ought to take a drive up there sometime and have a look around."

She thought about it for a minute. "I know! Let's go during spring break. We can rent a room close by and spend a couple of days snooping around. It'll be fun."

A week later we loaded up my van and made our way across the state line into western Pennsylvania, lodging in a cheap motel in Beaver Falls just a few miles from Apparatus Hill. Uncle Bud's old farmstead was virtually unchanged. There were more cornfields and an apple orchard now, but other than that, it was pretty much the way I remembered it. We slowly drove by, taking it all in. There were 'No Trespassing' signs posted on the old wooden fence, so we walked along the side of the road admiring the scenery until we came to the trail leading up to the old fishing hole. I recognized it immediately. "This way," I said. Nothing much had changed up on Apparatus Hill either. The pond seemed smaller than I remembered. We sat down in the tall grass where we could kick back and watch the cattle grazing in the fields below.

It was a gorgeous spring day, but I was starting to feel a bit uneasy.

"Hey, are you OK? You seem awfully quiet," Valerie asked.

"Sorry, I was just thinking. Maybe we should go grab something to eat and come back later?"

"Whatever you say. Are you sure you're alright?" she said, tenderly rubbing my shoulders.

"Oh yeah, I'm fine," I reassured her and got up to leave.

When we returned to Apparatus Hill just after nightfall, the woods were crawling with hundreds of those little gray toads. The pond was shrouded by an eerie bluish-green mist which swirled gently above the murky water. We trudged along the fishing hole, slipping and sliding through the mud, looking for anything unusual. "This place gives me the creeps," Valerie said.

"No kidding. When I was younger I used to come up here all the time to see how many bullfrogs I could catch just for fun."

"So what do you think is responsible for all those cattle mutilations?"

"Who knows. Probably some kind of wildcat. Maybe a pack of wild dogs."

We both heard it at the same time and stopped dead in our tracks, a smooth rhythmic sound coming from the other side of the pond. We pointed our flashlights in the direction of the noise, expecting to see a beaver or even a muskrat swimming around. But what we saw made us both gasp and quiver like porcupines. It was the 'Old Hagfish Lady' and she was standing up on a wooden raft tied together by vines just paddling slowly through the mist. She was a twelve foot giant and the very sight of her made me cringe. She was flaunting a cow head hide pulled down over her face with the eye sockets ripped out and its lips peeled back over its rotting teeth. It was easily the creepiest, most repulsive thing I had ever seen. The creature turned to look at us, and Valerie let out a terrifying shriek. I grabbed her by the hand and we took off running down the hill.

THE GRAVEDIGGER

My name is Shywood Green and I'm a gravedigger. I'm the first one to come and the last one to go when all the mourners have gone home to grieve. In my twenty plus years on the job I've seen it all, from corpses sitting up in their caskets to wild dogs digging up fresh graves and everything in between. At 6'2, 225 pounds, it takes a lot to rattle my nerves. But nothing could have prepared me for what happened on that cold and foggy night in early November.

It was right around quitting time and I was just finishing up for the day. Temperatures were dropping fast and Saint Alban's Cemetery was silent and still. It was getting dark and Willy, the backhoe operator, had already gone home for the weekend. I was working feverishly, putting the finishing touches on a grave we had dug earlier that morning, getting it ready for the marble headstone due to be delivered and set in place in three days. The body belonged to one Veronica Blackstone, a mysterious young widow allegedly involved with the occult who had evidently died under some rather dubious circumstances just days before. I remembered hearing the rumors circulating around town, something about the young widow being responsible for the recent disappearances of several schoolchildren from the local parish. At the time I really didn't believe a word of it, they were, after all, just rumors.

I could barely make out the silhouette of the old church and the crumbling tombstones, the fog was so thick. My fingers and toes were tingly and numb from working all day in the bitter cold. I sat down on a nearby tombstone, smoking and rubbing my hands together, when I heard a faint scratching noise coming from the widow's grave. It sounded like a raccoon or something clawing in the dirt. I took a flashlight from the Ditch Witch and went over to investigate. I slowly tiptoed around to the other side of the mound, but didn't see anything. No raccoon, no scratch marks, no nothing. I got down on my hands and knees on the half-frozen ground and pressed my ear against the grave. The scratching was coming from inside. Could rats or mice have chewed their way through the casket already? Or had we inadvertently buried the young widow alive? I slowly backed away from the grave. It gave me the chills. I tried to shake it off and convince myself that it was just my imagination playing tricks on me. I was fatigued. It had been a long day and I was anxious to get home. I packed up my stuff and got ready to leave when I looked over and noticed a peculiar red mist rise up from the widow's grave, swirling around in the fog like a floating pool of blood. Slowly the figure of a woman began to take shape. Blurred features formed on her face: A pointed nose, a crooked grin and a pair of sunken eye sockets staring blankly into the darkness. The specter called out to me from another dimension, softly whispering my name over and over, "Sshyywood... Sshyywood..."

An uneasy feeling of despair followed me all the way home. Inside, the house was cold and dark. I cranked up the heat, crawled into bed and slowly drifted off. The phantom lady stayed with me all through the night, pursuing me in my sleep, haunting my dreams and whispering my name over and over, "Sshyywood... Sshyywood..." I must have tossed and turned for a good part of the evening because at 1 AM I suddenly woke up shivering in a cold sweat and sat straight up in bed. Trembling with trepidation, I bundled myself up in blankets and cautiously made my way downstairs. The house was dark and quiet. Outside the fog was dense, a light steady breeze was blowing and the ground was coated with a fresh layer of frost.

I was alone in the house, or so I thought. The bedroom door clicked shut. Then I heard the familiar scratching sounds coming from the bedroom and the phantom lady's desperate cries as she whispered my name again and again, "*Ssshyyywood ... Ssshyyywood...*" I knew what I had to do. I grabbed my coat and hurried back to the cemetery. I climbed the twisting path through the darkness until I reached the widow's grave at the top of the grassy hill and started doing what I do best.

For what seemed like an eternity, I dug and dug, and didn't stop digging until I found the casket three hours later. I threw my shovel aside, got down on all fours and cleared away the remaining soil. I picked up my crowbar and pried as hard as I could. After several attempts, the lid gave way and flung open. I was appalled by what I saw. Or more precisely, what I didn't see. For the body of the young woman whom I thought we had accidentally buried alive was gone. All that remained was her empty casket. Horrified and confused, I stood up when something as light as a feather gently brushed against my shoulder. "*Ssshyyywood...Ssshyyywood...*" I whirled around and there she was, just hovering in the freezing fog like a relentless ghostly apparition pleading to be set free. She stretched out her hand and I recoiled instinctively. I stumbled backwards, tripped over my shovel and into the casket I tumbled. The lid slammed shut. I was trapped. I banged and kicked as hard as I could, but no matter how hard I tried, the lid refused to give way. From above I heard the sound I had been dreading the most: The first shovelful of dirt coming down on top of me. Then another, and another. I kicked and kicked and slammed my body up against the lid over and over, but it was just no use. I had to find a way out and fast, otherwise I would end up buried alive and nobody would ever know. In desperation, I bent my knees as far as they could go, and using both my feet, kicked the side of the casket with all my might. The casket split apart, splintering into pieces, and dirt started cascading in. I slid through the narrow opening and crawled up out of the grave. I looked around but there was nobody there. My shovel still lay on the ground right where I had tossed it moments before.

For the next two hours I worked feverishly filling in the widow's empty grave and smoothing out the soil. By the time I finally finished, the first morning light was beginning to glow on the horizon. I quickly gathered up my things and ran from the cemetery. I never spoke a word to anyone about my frightening encounter with the crimson lady that cold and foggy November night. Sometimes late at night when I'm sleeping, I can still hear her calling to me from beyond the grave, softly whispering my name over and over, "*Sshyywood...Sshyywood...*"

THE GHOSTS OF DRAGONHORN MANOR

Parthenia was just an orphan when she first arrived in Charleston in the summer of 1914 at the age of eighteen. Under the auspices of Professor Dragonhorn, Parthenia would live out the rest of her sweet short life hidden away in the confines of his stately Victorian mansion, where I was employed as the seasonal gardener.

By day, while Professor Dragonhorn was away on business or teaching at the university, Parthenia occupied most of her time studying in the private library under the care and guidance of her tutor, Penelope. When the weather was fair, I would often see Parthenia strolling leisurely through the garden, stopping occasionally to elegantly smell the roses in her beautiful silky flowered sundress, or galloping along on her young mare up and down the equestrian trail under the watchful eye of the handsome young stable hand, Jonathan, her long chestnut hair flapping wildly in the cool summer breeze blowing in from the bay.

Sometimes at dusk or early in the evening I would even spot Parthenia wandering around the old cemetery adjacent to the Dragonhorn Manor, her ghostly milk-white gown fluttering gently under the pale moonlight as she glided carefree among the crumbling tombs and moss-covered statuesque. We even exchanged friendly pleasantries on a couple of occasions. She was a dazzling sight to behold.

When Parthenia was just nineteen, she suddenly came down with a high fever after being thrown from her horse and knocked unconscious one hot summer day. The family physician was immediately dispatched to her bedside, as was the local parish priest, but it seems Parthenia had also suffered a nasty insect bite to her neck and passed away in her sleep three days later, her remains entombed in a private mausoleum at the old cemetery.

Clearly distraught over Parthenia's loss, Professor Dragonhorn's health gradually started to deteriorate and he fell into a deep depression, locking himself up in his chambers like a recluse for weeks on end. In the days that followed, Penelope and Jonathan were let go and Parthenia's cherished mare sold off. I stayed on as the gardener, however, receiving my monthly pay from Professor Dragonhorn's personal accountant as usual.

In remembrance of a young girl's life suddenly cut short by unspeakable tragedy, sometimes I would cut fresh flowers from the garden and place them by Parthenia's shrine. One afternoon I was working in the rose garden when I happened to look up and noticed Professor Dragonhorn watching me from the balcony window. It seemed a bit odd at the time, but I didn't really think much of it until the following day when he suffered a stroke or some kind of mental breakdown and had to be taken away by carriage to the hospice up on Bench Street.

It was on one of these frequent visits to the old cemetery when I believe I first saw Parthenia's spirit - A fleeting glimpse of a passing shadow gracefully drifting across the last narrow shaft of sunlight filtering beneath the entrance of Parthenia's tomb. Disturbed by what I saw, I set the bouquet down on the steps and started walking hastily toward the gates. When I reached the next row of graves, I suddenly found myself standing face to face with a pair of matching mausoleums. The massive stone monuments were impressive, identical to Parthenia's tomb, with the Dragonhorn family crest engraved at the top, and the names *Priscilla 1898-1918* and *Emily 1899-1917* inscribed in gold letters just below. I was a bit puzzled by this unexpected discovery and wondered how I had missed them all this time.

The next day I hopped the brand new trolley car downtown to see if I could dig up some information about the girls. I scoured obituaries and death certificates, sifted through birth certificates and announcements, but didn't find any records for a Priscilla or an Emily associated with the Dragonhorn Estate. A further search through the archives at the local historical society did, however, yield some black and white photos of two young girls who looked an awful lot like Parthenia. In fact, all three girls looked so similar that they may very well have been siblings. Attached to the pictures was a newspaper clipping which read: *Priscilla, age 19, died on October 13, 1918 from serious injuries sustained following an accidental fall down a flight of stairs in the Dragonhorn Manor. Emily, age 18, died on July 31, 1917 after being struck by lightning while playing outside the Dragonhorn Manor. Priscilla and Emily were orphans adopted by Professor George Dragonhorn from Vilnius, Lithuania. Both girls were buried side by side in the old cemetery near the Dragonhorn Estate.* I'm not one to believe in coincidences and I started to grow more and more suspicious. I may have come away with more information than when I started, but I was still left with more questions than answers. Not of least which, Professor Dragonhorn's interest in young girls. I feared the worst.

Later that night, just as I was about to fall asleep, I could have sworn I heard the sound of galloping hoofbeats outside my window. I dragged myself up out of bed and parted the curtains. The night was warm and muggy and the sky was overcast. It was too dark to see beyond the cemetery, so I slammed the window shut, closed the curtains and crawled back into bed, only to be awakened fifteen minutes later by the pitter patter of footsteps running up and down the hallway. I lit a candlestick, twisted the doorknob and peered down the long dark hallway.

When I reached the landing at the top of the stairs, I snuffed out the flame and flipped on the wall switch. Soft light from a pair of sconces illuminated the mezzanine in a gloomy glow. Outside the wind was howling, rattling the shutters. Hail started pelting the rooftop. I strained my eyes in the dim yellowish light and peered down the narrow flight of stairs. Suddenly there was a brilliant flash and a thunderous boom which shook the mansion to its very foundation and made me practically jump out of my skin. The lights flickered and the chandelier started swaying, as if somebody were playfully swinging back and forth.

When I got to the bottom of the stairs, another bright flash lit up the parlor and the house went completely dark. As I fumbled through my pockets for a book of matches, a violent gust of wind blew the front door wide open, slamming it hard against the wall with a terrible crash, nearly tearing it off its hinges. A monstrous looming shadow slowly crossed the threshold and crept its way into the parlor. I recognized the silhouette right away by its enormous size and shape, and the black lifeless eyes which seemed to stare back at me with hatred and shame through the darkness. Something tugged gently on my nightshirt. And from out of the darkness came the tormented screams of three very frightened young girls. Suddenly Professor Dragonhorn's angry demonic voice roared through the mansion, "Get out! Get out of here and leave us alone!" The proverbial black cloud hovered in the doorway for a moment, then came rushing toward me. I grabbed a poker from the hearth and blindly felt my way down the long dark hallway. I escaped out the backdoor and hid in the toolshed until a thunderbolt struck the stables and sent me fleeing foolishly in the direction of the old cemetery.

The wind was whipping around and branches were strewn about everywhere. I searched the grounds for a safe place to shield myself from the driving rain when a giant tree limb snapped and came crashing down just a few yards from where I was standing. It was much too dangerous to stay there any longer, so I decided to take my chances and head back inside before I ended up electrocuted or crushed by a falling tree.

I hurried down the footpath paralleling the equestrian trail when something odd caught my eye. It was a freshly dug grave, a mound of damp soil heaped in a pile just a few feet away, and a temporary grave marker that read: *George Dragonhorn*. Another magnificent flash split the night sky with a tremendous explosion, striking the stable and sending a shower of sparks cascading down onto the roof. The manor burst into flames and by the time the fire brigade finally arrived the entire structure was fully engulfed and burned to the ground, all of its dark sinful secrets of lust and betrayal buried beneath the tons of debris.

METRO ZOO

As soon as I saw her I knew she was one of them. I could tell by the way she carried herself across the busy intersection and strutted confidently past the old theater, blending in effortlessly with the lunchtime crowd. Like the rest of her kind, she was a beautiful yet subtle creature who probably led a solitary existence with very little social interaction to speak of except what would only be necessary to fit in comfortably with her natural surroundings. You see, I learned a long time ago, these types of creatures aren't really that difficult to recognize, you just had to know what to look for. She glanced over her shoulder at me as she whisked by the Gothic cathedral. A colorful carefree chameleon casually going about her business. I knew it wouldn't be long before the animal games began.

From my hotel room up on the 7th floor I had a clear view of the park blocks, the fountain, the carousel, the street musicians, and all the partygoers gathered in the coffee shops and nightclubs. I watched with vague interest as a steady stream of nightlifers shuffled in and out of the shops and restaurants that line the boulevard. That's when I spotted her sitting all alone sipping a tall drink outside one of the fancy cafes. Curious, I stood by the window and watched her for a few minutes. She tilted her head, looked straight up at me and grinned. I quickly closed the curtains, threw on my overcoat and rushed out of the room to the elevators. I dashed through the lobby, out the front doors across the park and busy boulevard. But she must have known I was coming for her because when I got to the cafe, she was gone. Her half-empty glass smudged with lipstick still stood on the table.

There was a small group of yuppies hanging out drinking beer nearby. I turned around and said, "Excuse me, but did any of you happen to notice which way the woman who was sitting here a moment ago went?"

Clearly annoyed that a complete stranger would have the gall to interrupt their little get together, one of them pointed in the direction of the park and said, "She went thataway, buddy."

But that was impossible. I had just cut through the park a moment before. I would have run right into her. "Are you sure?" I asked with uncertainty.

"Yeah, I'm sure."

For the next fifteen minutes I scoured the park blocks, searching for her in vain. For I knew she had vanished once again. Back to my suite I went, confused and exhausted, and realized that in my haste I had forgotten to lock the door. I gently pushed it open and peeked inside. The room was dark and empty except for my suitcase which still lay unpacked on the bed. Then I noticed my phone extension flashing red. The front desk must have called while I was out. I took the elevator down to the lobby and marched right up to the night clerk on duty. "Good evening. I'm Mr. Strauss from room 707. I believe you called me about something…?"

"Yes sir, I did," she replied pleasantly. "Somebody left you a letter while you were out." She reached down and handed me an envelope with my name and suite number written on it.

"But no one even knows I'm here," I said in a puzzled tone. "Did they leave their name or anything?" I said as I opened the envelope. It was a ticket to the Metro Zoo and it was dated for the following day.

"No name, sorry. She did say she'd see you tomorrow though. A secret admirer perhaps…?"

I chuckled and said, "Tell me, miss. Is this your handwriting by chance?"

"No sir, it is not. Your name and suite number were already on the envelope when she handed it to me."

"I see. And what exactly did this mystery woman look like, if you don't mind me asking?"

"No, not at all. Um, let's see. She was tall and slender. Exceptionally pretty, probably in her late twenties or early thirties, I would say, with long blond hair. Very pleasant."

It had to be the girl from the cafe. Who else could it possibly be? "Interesting," I mumbled. "One more thing. Do you happen to know if this secret admirer of mine is also a guest here at the hotel?"

"I don't think so, Mr. Strauss. I don't recall ever seeing her around before."

"Well thank you very much. You've been most helpful." I wondered if I was being lured into some kind of trap. But then I thought, what could possibly go wrong at a crowded zoo? I went back to my room and watched TV for a while before nodding off.

The following morning I hopped the 10 o'clock shuttle bus to the Metro Zoo. It was another beautiful sunny day and when I arrived there was already a long line of visitors waiting to get through the gates. I scanned the crowd to see if I could spot her waiting for me, but there was no sign of her anywhere. Inside the plaza, the gift shop and concession stands were packed full of young kids and moms and dads pushing baby strollers. I had to fight my way through a group of elementary school children just to get past the Primate House.

My first stop was the African Safari then on to a brand new exhibit that had recently opened featuring several species of crocodilians from three different continents. The enclosure was dark, muggy and extremely uncomfortable, like an Amazon rainforest. But the giant reptiles were quite impressive so I hung around there for a bit. Most of the crocs and alligators were just kind of suspended in limbo with their eyes protruding above the murky water watching the little children come and go, wondering which ones would be staying for lunch.

By the time I got out of there my clothes were drenched with perspiration and the sun was blinding my eyes. To my relief I spotted a vacant bench where I could sit down and cool off for a few minutes. As I crossed the path for the sanctuary of the shade, a scrawny looking boy, probably nine or ten years old, suddenly plowed right into me with a big wad of cotton candy in his mouth. I reached out and grabbed his arm to prevent him from falling to the pavement. "Oopsie daisy! Are you alright, kid?" He was wearing dingy khakis and an old tattered jean jacket. I stooped down until I was eye level with the boy and said, "You really must be more careful and watch where you're going from now on."

"Sorry, mister," he muttered. He seemed distracted and looked right through me. Something else had caught his attention. "Why is that lady staring at you...?"

I spun around to see who he was talking about, but there wasn't anybody there except a couple of maintenance workers and a vendor pawning souvenirs. "What lady...?" I said, but he had already darted off in the opposite direction. Let the animal games begin, I thought.

Behind me was the Aviary, and next to that the Reptile & Amphibian Complex and Conservation Center. She could have easily slipped into either one without me noticing. I searched the Aviary first, but she was definitely not in there. The Reptile & Amphibian Complex was a hexagon-shaped structure with lots of exotic plants and rows of terrariums full of frogs, lizards and snakes. There was even a separate enclave for venomous snakes where only children accompanied by an adult were allowed, so I checked in there, but nothing doing. I walked around full circle and still didn't see her anywhere. I knew she was watching me from somewhere, I could feel it in my veins.

Weary of her childish games, I started down the path toward the gates when I heard a woman's voice say, "Leaving so soon, Danny...?" I turned and there she was, my beautiful elusive butterfly, just sitting there all by herself on the bench with her legs crossed all ladylike, smiling up at me with that malevolent grin. She nonchalantly lowered her sunglasses and our eyes collided. Let me tell you, she was drop dead gorgeous in her green and yellow sundress and high heels. She had long, curly blond hair with pink and orange streaks, sapphire-blue eyes, and a black shawl draped across her shoulders.

I cautiously walked toward her. She watched with amusement

as I approached, luring me closer and closer. I should have run away right then and there, but I was drawn in by her hypnotic gaze. I sat down right next to her, never turning my eyes away. I could feel the hair on the back of my neck bristle, tickling my skin with a tingly sensation. "Do I know you...?"

"Would you like to?" she asked sardonically.

"I know who you are."

"Oh do you now...? Who am I?"

"What the hell do you want from me?" I snapped, already growing agitated by her carefree demeanor.

"Your undivided attention, what else."

"Is that so? You don't own me. I'm not some kind of puppet you can just manipulate anytime you please," I said vindictively. "So unless you have some immediate business with me, I suggest you stop spying on me and leave me alone!"

She uncrossed her legs, looked me straight in the eye and said, "My, my, my, Danny! There's no need to get all testy. That's no way to treat a lady on the first date."

"Stay away from me, I'm warning you. Or else I'll..."

"Or else you'll what...? Call security? Cage me like a wild animal? Have me removed from the zoo on such a beautiful day? That would be such a shame. Come on, Danny boy, you can do better than that. You ought to know by now, I don't frighten away that easy." She reached inside her purse, pulled out a makeup kit and mirror and started painting her lips, ignoring me as if we had never had this little conversation.

I stood up furiously and said, "That's it! We're done here. I'm leaving now. Goodbye."

"See you later, Danny. It was nice meeting you too," she cackled.

I turned to walk away. "Stay away from me, do you understand? I mean it!" But she just smirked and continued applying her lipstick. I checked to see if she was following me. The bench was empty. She had evaporated into the crowd without a trace.

When I got back to the hotel I noticed my suitcase had been

moved. There was a clean stack of towels in the bathroom, the bed had been made, and the carpet had been vacuumed. The maid must have come in and refreshed the room while I was out. Tired and hungry, I decided to take a quick shower and a short nap before heading down to the restaurant for dinner. I grabbed a set of clean clothes from my bag and went into the bathroom. In the mirror I saw something crawl out my suitcase and slither across the floor. I stepped out onto the carpet and a creature, which can only be described as a cross between a cobra and a millipede with hundreds of tiny fuzzy feet and antennae, suddenly lunged up at me, lashing its forked tongue and snapping its monstrous mandibles as it flew through the air toward my frightened face. I ducked and the creature slammed against the wall with a deafening crash and started hissing. With my back against the wall, I slowly crept towards the door in hopes of sneaking out into the hall and making a run for it. The creature coiled up in a ball, poised to strike again. It started to close in on me when the phone on the nightstand unexpectedly rang. I picked up one of my shoes off the floor and hurled it across the room, knocking the receiver off the hook. Bullseye! The receiver tumbled off the cradle and the clerk's concerned voice crackled through the speaker. "Send help!" I shouted. The creature retreated, scurrying under the bed. I rushed back into the bathroom and barricaded myself against the door. I heard the creature slam hard up against the door several times, then it stopped and everything got quiet. A few moments later the phone rang again. How was that even possible?

After what seemed like an eternity, I heard somebody banging on the door, "Mr. Strauss, are you in there...? It's hotel security...Is everything alright?"

"Yes, I'm here. But there's a snake in my room and I'm trapped in the bathroom. Please hurry!" I pleaded.

"Alright, stay calm. I'm coming in." I heard him unlock the door and enter the room. I cracked open the bathroom door and peeked around the corner. The creature was still under the bed. I stepped out of the bathroom with just a towel wrapped around my waist. I must have looked totally ridiculous standing there half naked as white as a ghost. "Um, are you alright, sir...?"

"Yes, I'm fine. Just a bit shaken. Now I insist you get me out of here at once!"

"Yes, of course. I'll get you another room right away. Please follow me, sir. I'll come back for your bag in a moment." I tiptoed over to the door, staying as far away from the bed as possible and hurried out into the hallway. He escorted me to a vacant suite just down the hall. "Please wait here while I notify the front desk and retrieve your bag. And don't worry, I'll check your bag thoroughly to make sure it's safe." He returned with my bag fifteen minutes later and I crawled into bed.

As I checked out the next morning, I was pleasantly surprised when the clerk issued me a full refund for my two night's stay and apologized for all the inconvenience. I hailed a cab to the train station and arrived about a half an hour early. I had a little time to kill before my train was due for departure, so I picked up the phone and dialed the hotel.

"Marquis Hotel, Valerie speaking. How may I help you?"

"Yes, I would like to speak to security please."

"Certainly. And who may I ask is calling?"

"Daniel Strauss."

"Oh, Mr. Strauss! I thought I recognized your voice. Let me put you through to security now. Please hold." *Sleepy elevator music*

"Good morning, Mr. Strauss! Are you home already?"

"No, of course not. I'm calling from the train station."

"Is everything OK, sir...?"

"Yes, everything is fine."

"Good! What can I do for you?"

"Well, I was just wondering. Did you search the room where I was staying?"

"Yes, I did. In fact, I just finished up a short time ago."

"Really? Did you happen to find anything unusual?"

"Well, Mr. Strauss, as a matter of fact, I did. Underneath the bed I discovered what appears to be some kind of odd-looking snakeskin." He paused for a moment then said, "As a procedure, we also reviewed the surveillance footage for the 7th floor and the only other person coming and going out of suite 707 yesterday was the housekeeper."

Exasperated, I grabbed my suitcase and boarded the waiting train. As it pulled away from the station I glanced out the window and there she was, my colorful chameleon, just standing on the platform waving and smiling up at me with that malevolent grin of hers. There was nothing I could do. I watched her gradually fade away into the background as the train accelerated and sped off down the tracks.

Made in the USA
Middletown, DE
04 September 2023